THIS IS A WORK OF FICTION.
ANY SIMILARITY BETWEEN REAL
PERSONS, PLACES, OR THINGS, AND THE
FICTICIOUS PERSONS, PLACES, OR
THINGS PORTRAYED HEREIN, IS
ENTIRELY COINCIDENTAL.

Order this book online at:
www.Amazon.com

Or for a signed copy
with free shipping:

johnregan2100@gmail.com

jreganjr@protonmail.com

Front Cover Illustration
Copyright © 2007 Michelle R. Morse

Published by John Regan, 2008
North Palm Beach, FL

ISBN : 978-0-615-23200-3

"John Regan's book, "Return of the Children" is an imaginary work of fiction but it clearly comes from the heart of a man of deep faith. The book's basic premise underscores who God is and who we are as His children. In a beautiful and imaginative way it pulls the reader into a deeper reflection on what it means when we say that God is the Lord of Life. Many of us have lamented the "abortion" of our future when a child is murdered in the womb and John's book makes that lament all the more real and tangible. This book presents a profoundly pro-life message in story form, I pray that it may be read by millions and hearts may be changed.

Bishop Joseph E. Strickland
Diocese of Tyler

"Return of the Children is not merely science fiction. My aborted babies visited me, just after I returned from a Rachel's Vineyard retreat. Their love and forgiveness is truly a gift from God. John, thanks for the beautiful and sensitive telling of the visitations. Dr. Alveda C. King, Director of African American Outreach, Priests for life.

"This book is hard to put down. John Regan has the gift to make you feel that you are actually witnessing the event that he is writing about."

Don Kazimir, Director Respect Life Office
Diocese of Palm Beach.

"Words cannot describe the emotions that I felt while reading your book. The power of forgiveness is an amazing gift from God. Any woman thinking of having an abortion should read this as well as any women who have had one."
Michele R.

"BRAVO, That was a humble story that moved me! I am not ashamed to say that I am a retired NYC cop that cried while reading the book. My brother Thomas Bosco picked up the book, and he began to read it and could not stop until he finished the book with a Kleenex. He received a bronze star in Desert Storm for bravery and you made him cry."
Richard Bosco

"Enclosed please find a check for three more copies of your book, Return of the Children. Your book brought me to tears more than a few times."
Cheryl

"I read your book within 2 days as soon as I received it. I couldn't put it down. It is wonderful and very powerful. It has inspired me to try harder to simply bring compassion and God's Love to the women at PP."
James H.

RETURN
OF THE
CHILDREN

JOHN REGAN

TO

THE GREAT MOTHER OF GOD,

MARY MOST HOLY

1

THE MISSION

Stretching thousands of miles into the endless limits of the starlit universe, a massive column of 40 million pilgrims came to a gradual and disciplined halt. Their mission, divinely ordered and joyfully accepted, was about to begin. Spontaneously, without word or gesture, they knelt and, with one voice, prayed through their leader, Carrie Brown.

"Father, we have sadly seen the warm glow of Your eternal life slowly fade as we approach earth. We know You are with us, but we can no longer see or hear You. We miss You. We are sad. Still, we are ready to begin the work You have ordained for us."

Carrie, a tall and gracious young woman of Caribbean ancestry, had received her soul from God in August 1972. However, she had lost her life six months later, on Feb. 23, 1973. After a moment of silence, she stood up, turned, and addressed her brothers and sisters.

"Behind me you can see the glow of earth. Beautiful blue oceans, rich green fields and valleys. White clouds blow gently in the wind. This is where we all were conceived. This is where we died. We never had the life Father planned for us. Our purpose was never realized. But now, in His mercy, we have returned. We will have very little memory of Father while we are here. Before each decision, you must pray. He will enlighten you. As humans, there will be times when you will become afraid. It will be a new experience, like this sadness that has surprised us so. Not all of us will be on earth at the same time. Those who remain here will be praying constantly. Now be still as Father's Holy Spirit fills you with knowledge for the mission."

Complete silence consumed the sea of human souls as they bowed their heads in humble adoration. A familiar voice began to speak.

"My dear children, you are here. Here where you had your first beginnings. It is here where my love created you and shared you with others. They rejected you. I now bring you back again. Your mission is to change their hearts. If you bring my love and mercy, you will be successful. If you bring bitterness and anger, you will fail. My Spirit abides only in love. Be love to those you seek."

Silence continued over the sea of young adults and children. Still kneeling with heads bowed, they appeared to be individually communicating with their Creator in a singular and unique way. Many toddlers were holding the hands of older children in a seeming need for security on this lengthy journey. Those in their twenties appeared to be monitoring the well-being of the younger teenagers, and many of the teens were hovering close to the preschoolers. There was an obvious sense of family emanating from their ranks. Gradually, one by one, they rose to their feet and assembled in perfect order, two by two. Carrie turned and faced the earth. Reflecting brilliant sunlight and turning at an almost undetectable speed, it seemed to beckon the pilgrims to return quickly. But as inviting as it was, discipline still ruled the divinely assembled column and no one moved without a sign.

At the head of the column stood an

impressive young man. He was slightly less than 6 feet tall and his face beamed a holy but determined expression. Carrie approached and asked, "Bill, are you ready to accompany your sister and return to your mother and father?"

Bill turned toward his younger sister, Maria, who was 5 feet 3 inches tall and weighed only half of Bill's 180 pounds, and repeated the question.

"Are we ready, Sis?"

"I don't know, Bill," Maria answered in a faint whisper as she cleared a tear from her eye. "I'm very anxious and I don't know how to handle it. I don't remember having ever been anxious before and I have never cried before."

As Bill reached out to reassure and comfort Maria, he was surprised to see his hand trembling.

Carrie stepped closer.

"Listen, both of you. Love for your mother and father will remove all your fears. Become love and go in confidence."

There was silence. Maria hesitated, trying unsuccessfully to speak, while Bill struggled with anxiety and indecision. Awkward moments passed. Carrie closed her eyes and prayed. Then quietly, as if suddenly receiving strength and inspiration, Bill turned and hugged Maria, glanced at earth, faced Carrie, and announced with a smile: "We're ready."

Carrie beamed with enthusiasm, took a deep breath, and stepped to the edge of earth's atmosphere. Stretching forth her hand, she pointed toward the United States and said, "Your parents need you, my brother and sister. Go courageously and bring them Father's love."

Suddenly, in a flash of light, Bill and Maria began to descend rapidly into the upper layers of the atmosphere. The wind began to move forcefully against them. In seconds, they were plummeting faster and faster, until they raced across the face of the earth from west to east at lightning speed. California rushed by as they descended through the cloud cover, emerging high above the beautiful Midwestern Plains states. Hundreds of meticulously plowed fields came into view as they rocketed across the Mississippi Valley, heading northeast. Moments later, two miles above the Chesapeake Bay, their forward speed began to slow. Maryland, Delaware, and then New Jersey came into view as they descended even further. In less than thirty seconds, they were crossing the Hudson River and slowing to a complete stop five hundred feet above a major highway in New York state. Wind-tossed and breathless, Maria exclaimed, "Wow! That was some ride!"

"Tell me about it," Bill responded. "It was awesome."

Slowly they began to move in a northerly direction as the temperature dropped rapidly.

"Bill, I think we're becoming more human. I'm getting cold."

"Me, too, Maria, but I'm not sure what to do about it."

Without warning, they began to descend toward a large city. The ground was coming up fast as they continued to move northward above the six-lane highway. Suddenly, Maria yelled, "Look, Bill. We just passed a sign that read, 'Albany, next five exits.'"
Gradually their speed dropped as they approached the tops of very tall oak trees. They moved away from the highway and into the countryside, still moving northward. Finally, they came to a complete standstill, hovering just above a school playground. In moments they descended and gently touched the ground.

Bill immediately reached out and took Maria's hand as they moved closer to each other. Anxiously scanning their surroundings, he whispered, "Wow, Sis, we're here."

"I know," she responded quickly. "But where is 'here'?"

"I'm not sure, but the sign said 'Albany,' so we must be in or near Albany, New York."

Beginning to shiver, Maria complained again, "I'm getting colder."

"Me, too, Sis; let's try and find some coats," Bill responded as he pulled his blue wool sweater sleeves down around his hands.

Jumping the school fence, they began to walk in the direction of what looked like a small shopping center.

"Look over there on the other side of the supermarket, Bill. I see a clothing store."

"I see it, too," Bill answered, and together they bolted across the side street. Bill walked in first and held the door for Maria. Immediately an elderly man approached and asked, "No school today, kids?"

Surprised, Bill answered, "School? We don't go to school. I'm 29 and my sister is 27."

"Gee," the storekeeper responded, "I wouldn't take you for over 16, 17 years old at the most. What's your secret?

"Slightly embarrassed, Bill answered

"Well, we live a very healthy lifestyle."

"True," Maria added. "Plus, we follow the commandments of God, and our consciences are clear, which keeps us in good physical and spiritual health."

"It also keeps us young," Bill offered.

"Oh, uh, I see," the shopkeeper replied in a somewhat confused manner.

"Can you direct me to the coats?" Bill asked.

"Yes. Men's overcoats will be on Aisle 5 and ladies' on the other side of the store in Aisle 14."

Maria quickly found her size and donned a pale blue parka with a hood and fur lining.

"How's this, Bill?" she called as she turned to face her brother.

"I'm over here," Bill shouted as he buttoned up a green windbreaker with a fleece lining.

As Maria walked to Aisle 5, she passed a sale sign indicating end-of-season discounts on all winter merchandise.

"Wow, Bill. Everything is on sale."

"Yeah, I noticed," Bill called back, "but I just realized we probably don't have any money."

Maria quickly checked her pockets.

"Yes, we do. I have . . . let's see, one hundred-dollar bill, plus three twenties. I have $160."
"Great," Bill responded as Maria walked down the aisle. "How much is your coat, Sis?"

"The tag says $79.99, but it's on sale at half price. So that means its $40."

"Super. And mine is $90, but at half price . . . that's just $45. So after tax, we'll still have about $70 left."

"Yup, that's right," Maria agreed. Then she had a thought and said, "Look in your pockets, Bill, and see if you have any money."

"I already did and I don't have any at all."

"Find everything ok?" the store manager interrupted.

"Oh, yes, sir, thank you, sir," Bill replied. "I'll take this windbreaker and my sister will take that parka."

"Ok, young man. Please step over to the checkout," the manager instructed.

As he rang up the sale, the manager asked casually, "Just visiting?"

Surprised by the question, Bill hesitated. "Uh, well, yes, you might say that we are visiting."

"Might say'?" the manager asked.

"Bill means we are here on business but visiting at the same time," Maria interrupted.

"Exactly," Bill agreed as he gave the change to Maria and headed for the door.

Safely outside on the sidewalk, they donned their new coats and zipped them up snugly as the temperature continued to fall.

"What time is it, Sis?"

"The clock on the corner says 1:30, Bill."

"Well, we have an hour and a half before prayer, and I don't have any instructions for activity between now and then," Bill noted. "Do you have any, Sis?"

"Yes, and it appears we're getting into the mission immediately. We must go to Albany Women's Clinic."

Bill was about to ask Maria whether she had directions when she held up her hand and bowed her head in silence. Moments later, she looked up and said, "I have directions now. We go to the end of the shopping center on Seneca Street and walk north eight blocks. Then we turn right on Tenth Avenue and walk straight for half a mile. Albany Women's Clinic will be on the corner of Tenth Avenue and Capitol Boulevard. We need to hurry, as we're supposed to be there before 2 p.m."

"Let's go," Bill replied. "That sounds like at least a 15-minute walk if we don't get any traffic lights, which we most likely will."

Bill and Maria quickly walked the eight blocks and turned right onto Tenth Avenue. Maria glanced at a newspaper box on the corner. The headline read: "SPRING SNOW TONIGHT."

"Bill, that newspaper says it's going to snow tonight. Doesn't that mean the temperature will dip to at least 32 degrees?"

"Wow, it sure does," Bill answered as he jumped from the street onto a high curb. "We'll have to look for lodging if it's going to be that cold."

"About another quarter of a mile and we should be there," Maria puffed as she tried to keep up with Bill's pace.

As they passed a hardware store, the clock in the window read 1:50.

"I see a sign," Bill called out. "It says Capitol Boulevard is one more block."

Moments later, a sign that said "Albany Women's Clinic" came into view above a building.

"There it is," Maria cried excitedly.

Out of breath, brother and sister slowed to a casual pace and cautiously approached the building. Until now, this had been nothing more than an address they had been instructed to find. But as they came within view of the front door, something unexpected happened. "Bill, wait," Maria said. "Don't go any closer."Why?" Bill panted as he tried to catch his breath.

"Something is wrong. I don't know what, but I

sense evil."

"But Maria, we know that evil can't harm us. Remember?"

"I know. But I think I mean the evil of fear. And we were told that we could experience fear."

"True," Bill responded. "But what are you afraid of?"

Suddenly the front door opened and an elderly man walked out. He appeared to be about 60 years old. Gray-haired and heavy-set, he walked with a limp as he headed for a dark gray sedan near Bill. As he passed Maria, he slowed and looked directly into her eyes, then Bill's. He seemed as though he was about to speak, but he then broke eye contact and continued toward the car. Once inside, he started the engine. Slowly the passenger window rolled down and he looked directly into their eyes once more. A frown appeared on his face, but then, without comment, he abruptly drove off.

"Wow. What do you make of that, Sis?"

"I don't know, but he gave me the creeps."

"Yeah, me, too, little sister. Me, too!"

2

THE INVASION

Forty million souls stood at spiritual attention as the moment to mobilize quickly approached. Anxiety swept through the ranks as earthly emotions began to replace heavenly peace. Carrie picked up on the epidemic and quickly tried to overcome the negative anticipations with gentle words of encouragement, but she was not successful. Therefore, kneeling down, she used the power given to her by God for the mission.

"BROTHERS AND SISTERS," she called in a thundering voice that penetrated thousands of miles of silent space. "REPEAT THIS PRAYER WITH ME:

"Saint Michael the archangel, defend us in

battle. Be our protection against the wickedness and snares of the devil. Rebuke him, we humbly pray, and do thou o prince of the heavenly hosts, by the power of God, cast into hell satan and all the evil spirits who roam about the world seeking the ruin of souls. Amen."

Instantly, a powerful divine peace penetrated every heart and spirit, turning the staging area into an annex of heaven. Silence resumed as Carrie stood and spoke.

"As you know firsthand, we are no longer in eternity. We are in time. We are experiencing many of those things that humans experience: fear, anxiety, pain, confusion, discouragement, sadness. And now the moment has arrived for you to return to the place of your conception. Some of your encounters will be hostile. Some of you will be rejected. If you pray constantly and keep yourselves in Father's presence, you will be safe. When you were conceived, you received a guardian who remained at your side until you were aborted. Father has called forth your guardians for this mission."

Immediately, one hundred thousand angels appeared in a great flash of light, illuminating the darkened universe. Magnificent, brilliant beauty adorned the faces of all the guardians, who, while remaining in eternity, were physically manifested for the benefit of the souls entrusted to their care. Great love burst forth from each angel, causing tears to flow from every pilgrim. Peace filled their hearts and great courage returned to the souls who were about to undertake their mission.

"Will all those from Los Angeles in the 1970s please come forward?" Carrie asked.

With extreme order and precision, one hundred thousand souls stepped out of the column and made their way to the aura of earth's atmosphere.

"Please look at me," Carrie requested as tears filled her eyes.

"This is the moment we have waited for. The love of our Father that we experience in Heaven will now fill you abundantly. It is given so you can share it with others. Remember, you will have human emotions, but you will not have an inclination to sin. You do not have Adam's fallen nature. But emotions will be with you for the purpose of the mission. Do not let them cause you to fail."

Carrie stepped to the edge of earth's atmosphere and extended her hand as she had done before. Immediately, immense light surrounded the thousands of pilgrims as their guardians prepared to escort them.

"Go, my sisters and brothers. Your mission has begun."

Suddenly, in a flash more brilliant than the sun, two hundred thousand streams of light exploded in a silent burst, each like a laser beam aimed at a specific target. Racing toward California at breathtaking speed, the pilgrims and their guardians looked like meteors with blazing trails that nothing could stop.

Carrie turned to the millions standing in line.

"Most of you will depart very soon. We must wait for instructions. For those of you who have expressed concern about guardians for Bill and Maria, be at peace. They are well-protected. There was an immediate need for them to leave ahead of schedule. A soul is in great danger of losing salvation, and they could be the instruments to save it. We will now pray for that soul and all others."

Carrie knelt, followed by the millions of pilgrims. Her face was beaming with the light of love as tears continued to fill her eyes.

"Dear Father, you have called us here to serve you. Please bless with great repentance those we seek in your name. Let the sufferings of

Jesus turn their hearts from all sin and help them to experience your love in those you are sending. Encourage them to accept your mercy and to no longer deny you access to their hearts. In patience and love, we await your further instructions. Thank you. Amen."

An immense "AMEN" filled the universe as the pilgrims stood and took their places in line.

3

DIVINE MERCY

Buried under mountains of new snow, Albany, New York, welcomed the warm spring sunrise that forced the frigid night aside. Sixteen inches of the unexpected surprise covered everything in sight of Lori Sullivan's large living room window.

"Bill, honey, come and look. There isn't a footprint anywhere. I don't even see a bird."

Bill Sullivan struggled to focus his eyes in the first few minutes of his day. Walking across the living room to the bay window, he surveyed their two-acre country home.

"Wow! I've never seen this much snow this late in April. Only a few days till May, and there must be at least a foot out there, Lori."

"Sixteen inches according to the radio, honey. The roads aren't plowed yet, and I guess that means we won't be going to work."

Bill and Lori owned a very successful children's clothing store. They stocked only the most expensive items, which were much in demand by their wealthy clientele. Between the two of them and one part–timer, they managed the operation six days per week.

Last week, however, their part-time helper, Connie Davis, had been hospitalized with pneumonia. Bill and Lori's daughter, Kathleen Sullivan, a medical student one month from graduation, was on spring break and had offered to help out at the store. Today was her day to open the store, but the snow made that very unlikely.

"Bill, honey, Kathleen will never get that little car of hers through this high snow. Maybe you better get the Jeep out of the garage so we can four-wheel it down to the store. In a few hours, the city streets will be cleared and she can relieve us so we can get back here and plow the driveway before dark."

"Sounds good," Bill responded with a yawn. Bill had never been a morning person and usually didn't "wake up" until after breakfast.

Across town in a student apartment complex, Kathleen Sullivan wrapped a scarf around the collar of her overcoat and stepped out of her front door into a small drift of snow. From her perch five steps above the ground, she could see that the first snow-plows had made an initial pass by the complex and the road was clear. Encouraged, she pushed her way through the drifts to her Toyota Corolla, which was sandwiched between two other cars but seemed fairly snow-free except for the top. Noticing that many other students had made a path to the highway with their cars, she decided to follow their tire tracks.

"Hope it's clear all the way to the store," she thought as she started the cold engine.

Minutes later, on the main drag to town, she noticed she was just about out of gas. "I'd better pull into this station before I run out," Kathleen murmured to herself, as she crossed lanes and entered the first island to fill up.

While the gas was pumping, Kathleen gazed around the station, noticing that it was also a small used-car lot with about ten cars for sale. An old SUV on the end of the first row seemed to have a window open. Kathleen could see two people sitting inside, one in the front and one in the rear. The snow was just about up to the bottom of the door, but there were no footprints in the snow. Kathleen couldn't understand how the people had gotten into the car.

"Could they have been in there all night, since before the snow started?" she wondered.

The pump stopped and Kathleen placed the handle back in its holder. As she walked inside to pay, she noticed a large snowplow barreling down the highway at a faster-than-usual speed. Just as it entered the intersection, a gray sedan coming in the opposite direction spun out of control and slammed into the snowplow, which flipped it over and crushed it.

"Oh, dear God," she screamed. "I hope no one is hurt."

Kathleen ran in to pay, hoping someone had called for help.

"Did anyone call 911?" she asked.

"Yes," the clerk at the cash register responded, "but they don't expect to arrive anytime soon. There are accidents everywhere and the snow hasn't been plowed in many areas." Back at her car, Kathleen became very concerned for the victims and decided to pull her car aside and see whether she could help.

"Surely there must be some medical help there by now," she thought as she ran down the plowed area of the highway. Traffic was at a complete standstill, as only one lane had been plowed in each direction.

"Is anyone a doctor?" a middle-aged woman screamed from the crowd gathered next to the crushed sedan.

No answer came.

"We have to do something," a young man called out urgently. "The person inside the car is bleeding heavily and will die if we don't help."

Kathleen panicked. "If I help, I could be sued if the injured person dies or is crippled for life," she thought. "I don't have insurance and I'm not yet licensed. Maybe they could charge me with a crime and then I might never get my license. All these years of hard work could go down the drain."

She remained silent but drew closer to get a better look at the victim. As she peered inside the car, the injured man looked directly into her eyes. He seemed to be pleading silently with her to help him. His look tore at her soul.

"This is what I've given my life for," she thought. "To help people. To save them from disease and injury. How can I just look when I can easily help? All I have to do is stop the bleeding and wait for the EMTs."

The victim, a man in his fifties or sixties, was pinned between the steering wheel and the back of his seat.The car was tilted at a 45-degree angle on its left side. The windshield was gone, and Kathleen could clearly see that a major artery on the right side of the man's neck was lacerated. Still in a panic, she looked back at the crowd, which seemed helpless and anxious for anyone to step forward and act. If nothing happened in the next minute or two, it would be too late.

Suddenly, in the midst of the crowd, there appeared a face that startled Kathleen. It was a young man who looked exactly like her father in his twenties. She had seen many pictures of her father in the albums at home when she was growing up. The young man seemed to be communicating with her, telling her to stop the bleeding, but he never spoke a word.

Suddenly, without thinking, she lunged through the broken windshield and applied pressure to a pressure point on the right side of the victim's neck. He seemed to sigh as soon as she touched him and his rigid posture began to relax.

"Don't worry," Kathleen said quietly, "I'm

a medical student and you have strong blood pressure at the moment. I don't know the extent of other injuries, but I don't see any other bleeding externally."

With her free hand, Kathleen began to probe the back of his neck, looking for signs of swelling or broken bones.

"Can you speak?" she asked.

No response.

"Can you blink your eyes?"

Frantically he blinked his eyes.

"Blink once for yes and twice for no," Kathleen instructed. "Do you have bleeding anywhere else that you know of?"

The victim blinked his eyes twice.

"Can you feel anything?"

One blink.

"In your legs?"

One blink

"In your arms?"

Two blinks

"Ok. You have feeling in your legs but not in your arms. You may have a broken back or neck, although I see no signs of a neck fracture. Can you breathe easily?"

Two blinks

"Is it painful to breathe?"

One blink

"I think you might have broken ribs or fractured vertebrae."

"Here comes Fire -Rescue" a woman shouted from the crowd.

Kathleen could hear the approaching siren and people yelling from a distance to clear a path for the EMTs.

"We should have you out of here and on the way to the hospital in a few minutes. Your blood pressure is still strong, so try to be calm."

"Let us by please," an EMT shouted to the curious onlookers. The young professional made his way through the crowd carrying his emergency medical case. Directly behind him was another rescuer pushing a stretcher.

"You a nurse?" he asked Kathleen as he reached the scene.

Terrified that she might say the wrong thing and be cited for practicing without a license, she replied, "No! I'm just trying to stop the bleeding."

"How did you know where the pressure point was?" he asked as he made his way inside the vehicle through the broken windshield.

"I read it in a trauma book," Kathleen replied.

"Can you keep your hand there for a

moment, I need to get his pressure."

"Yes," she assured him.

"Sir, your blood pressure is adequate," the EMT said. "We are going to get you out of here and to the medical center. Can you speak"?

"No, he can't," Kathleen replied. "But he can blink. He has feeling in his legs but no feeling in his arms. His neck seems ok, so he probably has back injuries."

"You sure know a lot for someone who is just trying to stop the bleeding. Are you a doctor?"

"No!" Kathleen replied again.

"Well, we're going to need some help getting him out of this wreck. Even though his neck seems ok, we are going to put a collar on him. Can you help us lift him to the stretcher?"

"I'll try. My name is Kathleen and I have some knowledge of how to move the injured."

"That's fine, but I will call the moves. We don't want to injure him further."

"Understood," Kathleen replied instantly.

"My name is Brian and my partner is Larry. We must use names when we speak so we don't confuse our moves."

"May I help?" a young man called from the crowd. "It will take at least four to move the victim."

"Thank you," Brian responded. "You sure can. What is your name?"

"Bill."

"Ok, Bill. Come on over to the driver's door and reach through the window. We need to move the driver's seat back as far as possible."

Once Bill was in place, Larry said, "Ok, Bill, I'm going to pick up the lever to move the seat. When I say go, I will push from my side and you can push from your side. Kathleen, you need to continue with that pressure point. Larry, if you can jump up on the hood and reach through the windshield, you should be able to steady his head as we move him backward. Ready everybody? . . . GO!"

The seat lunged backward, relieving the pressure on the victim's chest. His face twisted in agony as he moaned in pain.

"Ok, sir, we understand you are in pain," Brian said. "We can't give you anything yet, however, because we don't know the extent of your injuries. Just hang in there, we'll have you out of here in a few minutes."

Kathleen remained silent, as she could see that Brian was very experienced in trauma care and that this was an opportunity to learn and use the skills she had practiced in medical school.

"Larry, let's get a clamp on that lacerated vein on his neck," Brian ordered. "Kathleen, be ready to release the pressure."

"Clamped," Larry shouted back to Brian.

"Release," Brian ordered.

Kathleen pulled her thumb back from the victim's neck. Blood flowed slightly from the wound.

"That's Ok for now, Kathleen," Brian assured. "We need a little flow to eliminate clotting. His pressure is sufficient enough that we don't need plasma yet. Once we get him out of here, we'll start an IV."

"Understood," Kathleen shot back.

"Ok, everyone, it's time to move him," Brian announced.

"Bill, Larry and I will pick him up from under his knees while you place your hands under his shoulders and slowly turn his back toward you. Once his back is facing the door, we'll have to pick him up and pass him through the window. Ready. . . . Go!"

The victim immediately gave a loud moan as he opened his eyes wide and grimaced in pain. Where does it hurt?" Kathleen shouted. "In your legs?"

Two blinks.

"In your arms?"

One blink.

"Hold it," Kathleen ordered. "He now has feeling in his arms. Either we released suppressed nerves or his vertebrae are fractured and have twisted and opened the passage channel. If that is the case, we could permanently damage his back. We need to get a board under him before we move him any further."

"Where did you learn all that?" Brian demanded.

"I'm a third-year medical student just about to graduate."

"Well, why didn't you tell me before?"

"Because I didn't want to jeopardize my graduating by practicing without a license."

"Well, this is an emergency and I ordered you to help. You're just a bystander assisting me, the EMT in charge. I wouldn't worry about anything. I'm glad you're here. Larry, let's get a board under him. STAT."

Larry raced through the crowd, retrieved a trauma board from the ambulance, and raced back to the wreck.

"I think we'll need more help," Brian suggested.

"Agreed," Kathleen replied.

"We need some help moving this victim," Larry shouted to the crowd.

"I'll help," a young woman offered.

"Me, too," a clergyman replied.

Larry and Brian secured the board around the victim's back and shoulders.

"What about the collar?" Kathleen suggested.

"That's next," Larry answered.

"Ok! We need one man under each shoulder on the outside," Brian ordered.

Bill reached under the victim's right arm.

"Reverend, do you want to take his left arm?" Bill asked.

"Surely," the clergyman responded. "My name is Reverend Howard Jenkins."

"What about me?" the young woman asked.

"I'll need you and Kathleen on the outside ready to support the board as the victim is passed through the window."

"Ok, everyone, listen up," Brian ordered. "Bill and Howard have the arms. Larry and I have the legs. Kathleen and . . . I'm sorry, what is your name?"

"Maria," the young woman responded.

"Ok, Kathleen and Maria will support the board.

Remember, once we begin we do not stop until we have placed him on the stretcher. Ready. . . Go!"

Immediately Bill, Howard, Brian, and Larry picked up the victim and began to slide him through the window. Kathleen and Maria reached around Bill and Howard and placed their hands under the board as it emerged through the window.

"Hold it," Brian shouted as the victim's legs rested on the window ledge. Immediately he and Larry jumped out of the windshield and moved to the outside of the driver's door. Once they had the victim's legs secured again, they gently lowered him to the stretcher.

The victim was breathing heavier and faster than before, and Kathleen became concerned.

"His respiration is increasing and labored. We need to move him quickly."

"Understood," Brian replied.

"Clear a path please! Coming through!," Larry shouted.

The crowd stepped aside as Brian and his five helpers pushed the stretcher at a running pace to the ambulance.

4

BAD ADVICE

The Los Angeles Freeway was jammed with commuters as the Monday morning rush hour neared its peak. The time—8:25—flashed from the time and weather billboard just before the exit to Pasadena. Heading up the off-ramp, Nancy Klein maneuvered her new Volvo to the far right lane.

"Early for a change," she assured herself as she turned right and headed downtown. As traffic slowed approaching a red light, she picked up her cell phone and dialed The Woman's Health Center.

"Hi, this is Nancy Klein. I have an appointment at 2 p.m. today. Just checking to make sure you have me on the schedule."

"Yes we do, Nancy," the receptionist assured her. "Do you have someone available to drive you home?"

"Actually, no, I don't. Will that be necessary?"

"Yes, it will. You are almost four months pregnant and will be having a second trimester termination, which will cause weakness and some disorientation due to the anesthesia."

"Gee, I didn't know that. Well, I'll see if someone at work can pick me up. Ok, thanks. See you later."

Nancy noticed her pulse rate was somewhat faster than usual as she pulled into the parking garage beneath her office building.

Arriving right behind her was her former boss, Marty O'Shea. Marty was chief editor for the children's book division of New City Publishing and Nancy had been his assistant editor. Two months after being raped in the parking garage, she had asked for a transfer to sales and Marty had reluctantly approved. She had needed a rest, and sales had offered her some time away from her busy schedule. At least that was the reason she and Marty had given to those interested at New City. The real reason was her pregnancy and her subsequent decision to have an abortion. Working in the children's book division, with pictures of toddlers everywhere, had proved to be too much for her.

Only Marty knew of her plans. In fact he had suggested the abortion. He had two children of his own, but five years earlier his wife, Sarah, had undergone an abortion because they didn't want a third child. Now, fearing he would lose his star assistant permanently, he had suggested Nancy terminate her pregnancy also.

"Hi, Marty," Nancy called as she locked her car and headed toward the elevator.

"Morning, Nancy. Wait, I'll ride up with you."

As Nancy pressed the third-floor button, she noticed her hand was shaking.

Marty sat his briefcase on the floor as the elevator began to rise.

"How's it going?"

"Oh, the usual, Marty. You know. Another day in paradise."

Marty noticed the strained smile on Nancy's face.

The elevator stopped and the door began to open.

"Chin up, old friend," Marty encouraged. "There are better days ahead."

"Thanks," Nancy whispered as she made a

left and headed down the hall. Marty smiled and pushed "5" as the door closed.

"Gee, I hope she's all right," he thought. "She should be scheduled for that abortion any day now."

Walking into his office, he glanced at his family portrait on top of his desk. His son and daughter were both in college now. Suddenly, he recalled Sarah's abortion five years earlier. Marty sat down, spun his chair around, and propped his feet up on the window ledge. The sky and clouds usually gave him a sense of peace. As he stared into space, his mind wandered back to the abortion clinic on the other side of town.

He had driven Sarah there early one morning. They had barely spoken along the way. As he had pulled into the parking lot, she had begun to cry and had suggested they forget the abortion and go home. Marty had reminded her that they had already discussed it at length and had made a firm decision to abort the child. Sarah hadn't responded, but she had wiped her eyes, opened the door, and walked into the clinic. Marty had stayed in the car.

"To this day, Sarah still has nightmares," he thought as he put his feet down and turned toward his desk. Suddenly the phone rang, jolting him out of his daydream. "Marty O'Shea, good morning."

"Hi, Marty. It's Nancy. I'm scheduled for the termination this afternoon, and apparently I'll need someone to drive me home afterward. You're the only one who knows about this, so I really can't ask anyone else."

"Oh, uh, well, let me check my schedule Nancy and I'll call you right back." Marty spun his chair around and stared anxiously at the city skyline.

"Gee, I don't want to go back to that place again. Once was enough," he thought as his palms began to perspire. He also had been having nightmares, but he had never told Sarah.

Suddenly his pulse became elevated as he tried to figure a way out of Nancy's request.

"How did I ever get myself into this?" he thought. "I never should have suggested anything to anyone."

The phone rang.

"O'Shea."

"Marty, I need an answer," Nancy pleaded. She was quietly sobbing. Shocked, Marty bolted upright in his chair. In ten years, he had never seen Nancy cry.

"Oh, sure, Nancy! Sure! Sure! No problem!

I'll drive you home. What time?"

"About 1:45. They say I'll be free by about 4:00."

"Ok, Nancy, I'll meet you in the parking garage."

Marty hung up the phone and grabbed his water pitcher. He gulped down a half glass of water and began to pace back and forth in front of his desk. Becoming very anxious, he thought of calling Sarah and asking her what to do. "No, no that won't work. She'll just get all upset, and anyway I promised Nancy I wouldn't tell another soul."

Marty walked to the window and stared across town, his eyes resting on a large cross atop a steeple. The thought of praying crossed his mind, but he quickly rejected it. "How can I pray and ask God for help in getting out of driving Nancy to the abortion clinic? He would never suggest another person. He would just tell me to convince Nancy that it is a mistake and to cancel the whole thing. But then she'll panic and say she doesn't want anyone to know she's pregnant. They'll think she's been promiscuous and avoid her. Then she'll have to tell them it is a rapist's child, and some will say abort it and others will say don't. It will be a whole new nightmare. She also might mention that I suggested she abort the child, and that will ruin my reputation with all the working mothers on my staff."

Marty's breathing became heavier and faster. He was on the verge of one of his anxiety attacks. They happened whenever he was under extreme pressure. He sat down, put his head in his hands on top of his desk, and prayed.

"Dear God, please help. This is horrible. I don't know what to do. I just don't know what to do."

5

SAVING LOVE

"Albany General, this is Rescue 3. We are en route with a 60-year-old male with internal injuries. Pressure is low but stable. Pulse elevated. Minor shock. Suspect spinal injuries. He has a veinal laceration right side neck. Over."

"Roger, Rescue 3. What is your ETA?"

"At least 20 minutes with this snow."

"Begin fluids."

"Roger, Albany."

Brian hung the microphone back up on the overhang as Larry swung the lumbering rescue vehicle into the intersection and hit the siren. In seconds, they were racing at 40 miles per hour up the ramp to the Interstate.

"With only one lane open, we better pray

traffic is light," Brian suggested.

"Already got you covered on that one," Larry responded. "This guy doesn't look good. External injuries we can handle, but when it's internal, we don't know what we're dealing with."

"True," Brian agreed. "Kathleen, how is his pressure?"

"Stable but weak. He's starting to lose consciousness."

"Try to keep him awake, we need to communicate."

Brian jumped into the back and began an IV as Kathleen sat on a side bench directly adjacent to the victim. Occasionally he would look directly at her. He seemed to be trying to communicate.

"We are just a few minutes from the hospital. As soon as we get there, we will X-ray your back and neck and see what needs to be done. Try to stay awake so we can ask you questions. Can you still hear me?"

One blink

"Do you still have feeling in your arms?"

One blink.

"That is a good sign. You might have spinal injuries, but they probably can be corrected. Would you like me to pray for you?"

The injured man's eyes seemed confused. He didn't blink. Kathleen decided to pray anyway.

"Dear Lord Jesus, thank You for saving this man's life. Please reassure him of Your loving presence. Help him to put his trust in You. And heal him according to Your will. Thank You. Amen."

The victim stared at Kathleen and appeared somewhat sad as she continued to pray silently. She had been a devout Catholic since childhood. Her parents had sent her to St Patrick's Catholic School, even though they didn't practice their faith.

Suddenly she sensed a need in the victim to communicate. "Are you trying to say something?" she asked.

One blink.

"About your condition?"

Two blinks.

"About notifying your family?"

Two blinks.

"About praying?"

One blink.

"Do you want me to continue?"

One blink

"Specifically for you?"

One blink.

"Dear Lord Jesus, please help this man to speak so we can understand the nature of his injuries. Please let me know how to best help him. He wants me to continue to pray. I pray for his spiritual health, that he would know You and love You and wish to serve You. Please forgive him for his past sins and bring peace to his soul. Help him to forgive all those who have injured him in any way during the course of his life and please inspire those whom he has injured to forgive him. Help him to accept his current condition and offer his suffering to You for the conversion of sinners just as You offered Your suffering to save all souls, including mine and his."

Kathleen paused as she noticed tears coming from the victim's eyes. She reached for a tissue and gently wiped them away. Immediately, many more tears emerged, and she decided to let him weep for the good that it might be doing.

The siren began to wail as the ambulance approached a major intersection in downtown Albany.

"Two more blocks," Brian announced over the speaker.

Kathleen put her hand on the victim's forehead and made the sign of the cross with her fingers.

"In Jesus' name, be peaceful."

The victim closed his eyes momentarily as though accepting Kathleen's suggestion.

Suddenly, the doors swung open and emergency personnel reached in and grabbed the stretcher, rushing the victim into the emergency room. Kathleen was left standing at the back of the ambulance, hesitating to go inside lest she be questioned.

"It's Ok," Larry assured her. "People ride with us and help occasionally. We don't question them or hold them responsible for anything. Besides, you didn't do anything that Brian didn't order. You're fine. Relax."

Kathleen sighed with relief and followed Larry into the ER. Two doctors and several nurses were already examining the victim. Larry produced the victim's ID and handed it to Brian, who walked to the intake window and presented it to the woman on duty.

"We'll call his family right away," she announced as Brian walked back to the ambulance with Larry.

"Kathleen," Brian called, "is there someone you can contact to drive you back to your car?

Regulations prohibit us from transporting you anywhere."

"Oh, sure, Brian. Yes. Thanks, I'll call my mom."

Kathleen spotted a telephone down the hallway from the ER. Fortunately, it was a free house phone. Her purse was still in her car back at the intersection and she didn't have any change in her pockets. As she dialed the number, she caught sight of a wall clock above the phone.

"Good grief. It's already 10:30. Mom will have a fit the store isn't open."

After five rings and no answer, Kathleen decided to dial the store.

"Sullivan's Corner, may I help you?"

"Mom, it's Kathleen. I'm glad you're there."

"Oh, hi, honey. Don't worry about coming in until later when the roads are plowed. Dad and I drove the Jeep in."

"Actually, Mom, I did try to get in, but there was a terrible accident and I helped the EMTs with the victim. I'm at the hospital now and need a ride to my car."

"Are you ok, were you involved?"

"No, I wasn't involved, and yes, I'm fine."

"Ok, I'll send Dad right away to pick you up. Are you at Albany General?"

"Yes. I'll be waiting at the Emergency Room entrance."

"Ok, he's on his way."

Kathleen hung up the phone and walked toward the ER. Slowly her mind replayed the accident scene.

"Who was that young guy who looked like Dad's picture thirty years ago?" she murmured to herself.

Suddenly, a voice on the public address speaker said, "Dr. Murphy, ER. Dr. Murphy, ER."

"Dr. Murphy?" Kathleen repeated. "He's a heart surgeon. They usually don't do cardiac surgery in the ER. Trauma care maybe, but not surgery."

Just as she approached the ER entrance, the elevator across the hall opened and Dr. Murphy bolted out. As he ran into the ER, she noticed the victim from the accident being wheeled into the trauma operating area. Dr. Murphy followed and immediately went to a scrub sink.

"Uh oh, that is not a good sign. He must have broken bones in the heart cavity," Kathleen thought.

"Excuse me, miss, are you a family member?" the office nurse demanded. Surprised, Kathleen responded apologetically.

"Uh, no. No, I am not. I was just checking on a victim from an accident I witnessed."

"Well, I'm going to have to ask you to wait in the lounge."

"I'm sorry," Kathleen offered, "I didn't mean to break the rules. How is that man?"

"He has serious internal injuries. What specifically I don't know, but if you wish, I'll keep you posted."

"Oh, that's ok. Thank you, anyway. I have to catch my ride."

Kathleen walked into the warm sunshine as the water from the rapidly melting snow ran past her boots toward the storm drain.

"Dear Lord. Please help that man. And send his family to be with him."

Kathleen closed her eyes and contemplated God's merciful love. She tried to envision Jesus watching over the victim, but she was jolted from her peaceful prayer by the familiar sound of the Jeep's horn.

"Hi, honey. Hop in," Bill called.

"Hi, Dad. Boy you got here quickly."

"Well, it wasn't bad really. Most of the main roads are plowed and the rest are melting fast. Where is your car?" Bill asked as he spun the Jeep around the entrance circle.

6

TIME AND ETERNITY

Powerful anticipation swept through the ranks as 38 million children quickly assembled on the edge of earth's atmosphere. An equal number of guardian angels suddenly appeared, taking up positions beside each returning child. The massive invasion of love and mercy was about to descend upon all of the cities in the United States—except one.

"Please! I Need your attention," Carrie announced to her fellow pilgrims.

"Almost two million of us will remain here in constant prayer to support you. Listen to and trust your guardians. You will not ordinarily see them while on earth. However, there will be special circumstances when their presence will be visible to you; but only you. Therefore, do not speak of them to anyone. No one will believe you."

Carrie knelt, followed by 76 million children and angels. All bowed their heads in humble reverence. The glow of earth began to fade. The stars grew dim. The sun gave no light. Powerful silence consumed the universe.

Slowly, above the earth, a loving light began to appear. A gentle voice spoke.

"My children. I bring you My Son. His love will save those you seek. I will remain with you and bring Him to you whenever you call. Fear not. Be at peace. See His merciful heart calling you to victory."

Hundreds at first, then thousands, then millions began to raise their eyes, and a tumultuous roar of praise, love, and worship ensued. All arms were raised in adoration as the multitude cheered the child Jesus, held in the arms of His mother, Mary, The Queen Of Heaven and Earth. Carrie was ecstatic as she reached out in praise to Jesus. Then, the sea of souls instantly stood as Mary pointed to earth and said, "Save your brothers and sisters, my children."

In a blinding flash of light, millions upon millions of God's creatures descended into the atmosphere, propelled by the command of the Mother of God. The sun burst into view, the stars were reborn, and earth beamed with light as the pilgrims raced to every corner of America.

Carrie could not take her eyes off the child Jesus as He smiled with great love in her direction. Tears filled her eyes as she repeated, "Thank You, thank You, thank You." Carrie had longed for this moment for thirty-one years. She knew her mother had been agonizing over her abortion but had never sought forgiveness. Now Carrie would be able to visit her and try to convince her of God's great love and mercy. But she would have to wait for the appointed time. For now, she and the almost 2 million remaining children would pray constantly for the army of souls about to touch down on the earth.

One by one, like human raindrops, they landed in every conceivable circumstance and place: parking lots, fields, highways, office buildings, homes, schools, stores, courthouses, buses, planes, jails, battlefields, ships, farms, abortion clinics, hospitals, street corners, churches—wherever it was necessary for them to meet those whom they had been sent to save. No one witnessed their arrival except their fellow pilgrims and guardians. But, almost immediately,

encounters began to take place between the
children and their parents everywhere in America.

In a suburb of Houston, Texas, a young man
reading a morning newspaper while waiting in a
dental office heard a tiny child call out, "Hi,
Daddy."

Surprised, he pulled the paper aside to see a
little boy standing beside his chair. The child
reached up, put his tiny hand on the young man's
arm, and said, "I love you, Daddy."

Stunned, the young man replied, "I'm not
your daddy, little boy. I don't have any children.
I'm not married."

"I forgive you, Daddy."

"Forgive me for what?"

"Look at me, Daddy," said the tiny child,
staring directly into the young man's eyes.

"Who are you, little boy? " the man replied as
he straightened in his chair and put the paper
down.

"Keep looking at me, Daddy," the child said.

"Why do you want me to look at you? I mean,
I mean. . . ." Suddenly the young man's eyes filled
with tears as he began to recognize similarities
between the child's face and his own. He became
very anxious and afraid.

"Don't be afraid, Daddy," the child said.

"I came to forgive you for having me aborted. I came to forgive Mommy, too."

"You can't be . . . where did you come from? Am I just imagining this?"

"No, Daddy. I am real. I came from heaven. I am 5 years old. God our Father loves you. He knows how unhappy you are and wants you to be free from guilt and remorse. He forgives you and wants you to spend some time with me. You are His child, too. Pick me up, Daddy, I want to hug you."

"I . . . I don't think I can. I'm too afraid. I. . . ."

The young man began to sob and put his hands over his face. The little boy pulled himself up on the arms of the chair and tried to put his tiny arms around his father's neck, but he began to slip.

"Help, Daddy, I'm falling."

Instantly his father grabbed him and hugged him close to his chest. Sobbing, he struggled to speak. "I'm sorry, I'm so sorry. . . . I didn't know what to do. I wasn't married, and she and I . . . didn't want to have a baby. I just . . . can't . . . find . . . peace. I'm so sorry. Please . . . please forgive me."

"I do, Daddy. I do forgive you. I want you to be happy. We can play for a few days. Father said it is ok. Will you play with me, Daddy?"

"Yes . . . yes. We can play right now."

Abruptly, the young man stood and, still embracing his child, walked to the desk and said, "Excuse me, I will have to cancel and come back at another time."

7

DEFENDING LIFE

Marty had been praying on and off for almost four hours. His anxiety refused to depart, but the clock on his desk insisted he get his coat and head for the parking garage.

"I can't keep Nancy waiting," he thought. "I'd better get down there a few minutes early."

When the elevator stopped at the parking garage, Marty bolted down the ramp. As he rounded the last turn, he was shocked to see Nancy waiting by his car.

"Nancy, how long have you been here?"

"Just a few minutes, Marty. I couldn't stay in the office another minute. I've never been so anxious. This is the most horrible thing I've ever done in my life. I can't believe it is happening.

Somebody raped me and now I'm pregnant. I'm a mother. I'm having a baby. In four hours I'll be a murderer. Why did God let this happen to me?"

Marty jumped behind the wheel and opened the door for Nancy. As he started the engine, he turned and said, "Nancy, I have been praying all morning. Maybe God doesn't want this to happen."

"Well, then, why did He allow me to be raped?"

"I don't know, but I know there is an answer to this problem that He agrees with. We just haven't found it yet."

"Marty, you're not suggesting I keep the baby, are you?"

"I'm not suggesting anything, Nancy. I want you to be happy and I will do whatever it takes. Look—we will be driving for about twenty minutes. Maybe we could pray a little bit. What do you say?"

"Fine with me. You'll have to do the praying, though. I don't know any prayers."

"Ok. I'll pray for both of us. I'm Catholic, although I haven't been practicing for at least ten years. So we will just have to go with the prayers that I remember."

"It's the spirit of the thing that matters,

Marty. I'm fine with your prayers. Go ahead. I'll listen."

Marty spun the car down the ramp and onto the parkway.
He took a deep breath and began.

"Our Father, who art in heaven. Hallowed be Thy name. Thy kingdom come, Thy will be done, on earth as it is in Heaven. Give us this day our daily bread, and forgive us our trespasses as we forgive those who trespass against us. And lead us not into temptation, but deliver us from evil. Amen."

Nancy was silent. Marty turned just as she wiped tears from her eyes. His heart sank.

"Gee, Nancy. Maybe you could postpone it another week."

"Marty, I can't go another day with this agony. Either it's now or never."

Marty was speechless as they merged with traffic and headed toward The Woman's Health Center.

"If there really is a God and He does answer prayer, then maybe He will give me some sort of a sign, Marty. I just need something. Something substantial to signal what God wants of me. I'm so anxious I feel faint."

"Nancy, what would happen if you decided

to keep the baby, at least through the pregnancy, and then put it up for adoption?"

"What would you do, Marty? What would you do if you were pregnant and the child was a result of rape? Would you consider adoption knowing that you would never forget that your child was out there somewhere and you would never be able to see it or communicate with it?"

"True, Nancy, but what will you do if you can't forget that your child is dead and you were the cause? Every time you hear a baby cry you'll have feelings of guilt. Maybe you'll have nightmares for years and never want to marry and have children.
Maybe you'll have to seek an expensive counselor. I don't know, Nancy, I just think adoption would be better for you."

"Well gosh, Marty! What are you saying?"

Nancy burst into tears and began to weep uncontrollably.

"I'm sorry, Nancy. I'm just trying to help. I won't say another word. This is your decision."

Ten long and silent minutes later, Marty turned onto the off-ramp and headed toward the clinic. Before long, he pulled into the parking lot and was directed to a spot by a female escort. Nancy was ashen and silent. The escort approached the car, but just as she was about to open Nancy's door, Marty set the automatic door locks.

"Just a minute please. We will be with you shortly," he instructed through the closed window. The escort nodded and backed away a few feet.

Suddenly Nancy heard singing. She turned and looked across the street. There on the sidewalk were a dozen or so adults holding up signs: "ABORTION HURTS WOMEN," "YOUR BABY LOVES YOU," "WE CAN HELP," and "ADOPTION NOT ABORTION." An elderly woman was waving a brochure in Nancy's direction, motioning her to come out onto the sidewalk to talk. The escort tried to distract the woman, but she just continued. "PLEASE," she called. "WE CAN HELP YOU! SAVE YOUR BABY! WE LOVE YOU!"

"Marty, why are these people here?" Nancy asked plaintively.

"They're protesters. They are trying to convince you and other women to keep their babies and not abort them."

Confused and anxious, Nancy put her hands to her head and said, "A decision is a decision and I have already decided, so let's get this over with."

As soon as Marty opened his door, the escort opened Nancy's door.

"Welcome to The Women's Health Center" she said. "My name is Zelda. I'll walk you to the door."

"WE CAN HELP YOU. OVER HERE . . . SEE WHAT A PICTURE OF YOUR BABY LOOKS LIKE NOW. WE LOVE YOU," the elderly woman shouted across the parking lot.

Nancy stopped and looked at the pictures the woman was holding up.

"Don't speak to them. They are troublemakers," Zelda insisted as she pulled on Nancy's arm.

Nancy objected and pulled away from Zelda.

"PLEASE, WE JUST WANT TO HELP YOU," the elderly lady called. "COME AND SEE WHAT SIZE YOUR BABY IS."

"You'll be late for your appointment," the escort insisted.

Suddenly the protesters knelt down on the sidewalk and a young man passionately prayed, "DEAR JESUS, PLEASE HELP THIS WOMAN TO LOVE HER CHILD AND SEE THE TRUTH. PLEASE HELP HER TO SEE THE TRUTH."

The elderly woman stood up and held out

the pictures to Nancy. "Here, look," she said. "They won't tell you the truth inside the clinic. How many months pregnant are you?"

"It doesn't matter," Nancy replied. "It is still only tissue."

"No! No! That isn't true. Here . . . see a picture of a baby at eleven weeks. See the arms and legs and head. This is a baby."

The escort grabbed Nancy's arm and started pulling her toward the door.

"Let Go!" Nancy shot back and pulled away again. Then, turning to the elderly woman, she said, "Let me see those pictures."

"We can't come on the property or we will be arrested," the elderly woman complained. "Please come out here on the public sidewalk."

As soon as Nancy reached the sidewalk," she was surrounded by six members of Pasadena Right to Life.

"I'm Patti," the elderly woman offered as she handed the three-month gestation picture to Nancy.

Nancy gasped as she looked at the tiny but nearly complete human being in the picture.

"They told me it was just tissue and not formed yet, and this is only three months?"

"How many months pregnant are you?" Patti

asked.

Nancy remained silent as she continued to stare at the picture.

"How many months?" Patti asked again.

In a faint whisper Nancy said, "Four."

Slowly Patti handed Nancy a picture of a four-month baby. "This is what your baby looks like."

Nancy held the picture in her hand but tried not to look at it.

"Go ahead, we love you. It's Ok to look." Patti insisted.

Nancy turned her head and stared directly at the perfectly formed and complete child in the picture.

"Oh! Oh!" she screamed as she lost her balance and started to fall. Immediately the pro-lifers supported her as she cried, "This is a baby! This is a baby, not tissue. They lied to me! They lied to me!"

Furious and with fire in her eyes, Nancy stormed to the entrance of the clinic. Pulling the door wide open, she bolted directly down the hall and into the office of the startled director, Emily Hahn.

"Mrs. Hahn!" Nancy screamed. "You lied to me! This is a picture of a four-month baby! You told me it was just tissue! It is *not* tissue, it is a baby," Nancy insisted as she tried to wipe the tears streaming down her face.

"Nancy, it's Ok. It's Ok. Come on, let's go home," Marty's meek voice whispered over the shouting.

"Hello, Mr. O'Shea. Please, will you calm Nancy down? The patients are becoming disturbed," Emily pleaded.

"What!! How do you know his name? Marty, what is going on here? Have you been here before?" a furious Nancy demanded.

"Well, Nancy . . . it doesn't really matter. Please, let's just go home."

"Doesn't matter? Of course it matters! Everyone has been lying to me, including you, Marty."

Nancy stormed out of the director's office, stopped in the waiting room, and screamed, "All of you have been lied to! There is a real baby inside of you! Go outside and get a picture from those protesters."

Outside in the parking lot, Marty was speechless as he fumbled for his keys. Nancy walked directly to the pro-lifers.

"Thank you for saving my baby," she cried as Patti and the others embraced her. Moments later, two more women left the clinic and approached the pro-lifers for pictures.

Still sobbing, but with a victorious smile, Nancy walked to the car. As Marty nervously held her door open, she looked him directly in the eye.

"Marty, I want an explanation. I want to know why you suggested I kill my baby. And I want to know why these people recognize you. Marty started the car and exited the parking lot. Moments later, he noticed his voice trembling as he tried to answer Nancy.

8

INTERVENTION

Tom Murphy had been a surgeon for twenty-six years, and for the last fifteen he had been specializing in cardiac care. He rarely performed emergency surgeries, as most of his procedures were planned elective operations. But today he was facing one of those rare exceptions in the trauma room of the ER at Albany General.

A very meticulous and exacting individual, he did not like working with people who were not proficient and experienced in heart surgery. But this operation was shaping up as a vast departure from his preferred working conditions. With no time to move the patient upstairs to the cardiac unit, he was faced with performing immediate trauma surgery to the most significant organ in the human body—the beating heart.

"Let's go," Dr. Murphy instructed the anesthesiologist as the team of emergency-room physicians and nurses approached the table.

"The patient has fractured ribs in the heart cavity, and any pressure from one of us in the wrong place could cause full arrest. Do you all understand that?" Dr. Murphy asked.

"Yes, Doctor," the team members answered in unison.

Slowly the anesthesiologist turned the valve and administered the gas to put the patient "under."

"Ok. Ready," Dr. Murphy instructed as he watched the monitors. "Scalpel."

With one incision, he announced "We're in" and ordered clamps to stem the bleeding. After several more incisions, the patient's entire rib cage was exposed.

"The aorta is slightly punctured by a broken rib. We have to remove it completely to make room to suture," Dr. Murphy ordered.

Jim Owen, a senior staff ER trauma physician, moved in with large forceps and a battery-powered hack saw. He handed the forceps to a nurse and began to cut the bone as she held it in place. Suddenly the blade cut through the bone and deeply into the artery.

Instantly Dr. Murphy shot his hands into the patient's heart cavity and shouted "Sutures." As he frantically tried to sew the severed artery amid the heavy bleeding, the pressure from his hands on the rib cage caused another broken rib to continually hit the beating heart muscle.

"Arrhythmia," the anesthesiologist announced.

"Stand by paddles," Dr. Murphy shot back.

Suddenly a nurse's hand reached in and pulled the rib cage away from the heart with a strength that most men could not have managed.

"Good! Good! Hold it just like that for another minute if you can," Dr. Murphy pleaded.

"Yes, doctor," the young voice responded.

"Pressure dropping," the anesthesiologist dutifully reported.

"Just another thirty seconds and I'll have it," Dr. Murphy assured. "Keep holding nurse."

"Yes, doctor," she replied in a strangely calm and peaceful tone.

"Got it!" Dr. Murphy rejoiced as he withdrew his hands from the heart cavity. "Thank you, nurse. Thank you very much. I believe you saved the patient's life. What is your name?"

"Maria."

"You must be new. I don't remember that name."

"Yes, doctor."

"Dr. Owen, is the orthopedic surgeon here yet? We have four fractures to set," Dr. Murphy urgently asked.

"Yes. Dr. Jamie Coleman is scrubbing now. He'll be just another minute or so."

"That's great! By the way, what do we know about the patient?

"He's an OB/Gyn at Albany Women's Clinic. Sixty-two years of age. His automobile was hit by a snowplow."

"Albany Women's Clinic?" Dr. Murphy responded with disdain in his voice. "That means he must be an abortionist."

"Maybe so," Dr. Owen replied, "but he is still our patient and we have to save him."

"I know, I know, and we will. It's just that we're supposed to be healers not killers."

"Here comes Dr. Coleman now," Maria announced.

"Hi, Jamie."

"Hey, Tom. What do we have?"

"Four rib fractures. I had to sever a fifth in

order to suture an artery. I'm not sure if you can save it or not."

"Too risky, any pressure could dislodge it and cut that artery again. He can live without it," Dr. Coleman replied.

Satisfied, Dr. Murphy ordered, "Let's go," and the team reassembled to assist Dr. Coleman and complete the operation.

9

REFLECTION

Bill Sullivan maneuvered his Jeep alongside Kathleen's Toyota, which was now completely blocked by plowed snow.

"Oh no, Dad! Look at the pile of snow around my car."

"Don't worry, sweetheart. I have a shovel and I'll clear a path in the front. It'll take only a few minutes and you'll be on your way."

As Bill shoveled, Kathleen began to recall the accident and the people involved. Suddenly, the young man named Bill, who looked just like her father in his twenties, came to mind.

"Dad, there was a young guy at the accident who looked just like you did when you were in your twenties. I remember the pictures of you and Mom in the album on the coffee table. And now that I think about it, his name was Bill."

"Wow! That's weird," Bill responded as he panted for breath.

"Yeah, I know. He even had some of the same facial expressions that you have. I know he couldn't be a nephew because you were an only child. And he couldn't be a second cousin because all of your first cousins had girls. Pretty weird."

"Yep. Sounds weird all right," Bill responded as he continued making a path in front of the car.

"I think that's enough in the front, Dad. Now just a little by the rear tires and I should be able to move out."

"OK, sweetheart, just a few more scoops," Bill grunted as he shoveled under the car. "Now! Try that."

Kathleen opened the door and started her 10-year-old Corolla. Immediately the car lunged forward and out of the snow onto the plowed shoulder of the highway.

"Great, Dad. We did it. Thanks. I think I'll head to the store now and relieve Mom."

"Ok, Kathleen. I'll meet you there. Drive carefully."

As Kathleen pulled onto the highway, she

looked in her rear-view mirror to see whether Bill could get the Jeep out of the snow pile he had pulled into. Suddenly, she noticed that the SUV the two people had been sitting in at the gas station was gone.

"Hmmm. That was a strange situation," she mused as she tried to recall the scene. Suddenly she took a deep breath. "Oh Wow!! Those people in the SUV were the same people who helped at the accident—that guy Bill who looks like dad and the young lady who helped with the victim. What was her name? I can't remember. Gee, I wonder if I could find out who Bill was from the ambulance records."

As Kathleen reviewed the accident and all that had transpired since, she monitored Bill's progress behind her as they made their way across town.

Maintaining a safe distance behind Kathleen because of the slippery road conditions, Bill thought, "Three more blocks and I'll pull into the alley behind the store and let Kathleen have the plowed spot out front." Anticipating at least a foot and a half of snow in the driveway, Bill downshifted and put the Jeep into four-wheel drive.

Kathleen passed the store, made a U-turn

at the next intersection, and pulled right up to the front door. Moments later, the jingling doorbell alerted Lori that someone had entered the store, and she walked out front to greet the first customer of the day.

"Hi, Mom," Kathleen piped as she closed the door.

"Oh, Kathleen, sweetheart, I thought you were a customer, but I'm so glad it's you instead. Are you Ok? You must be cold and wet!" Lori exclaimed as she rushed to hug her only child.

"Actually, no, Mom. I'm Ok. Dad drove me back to my car and everything is fine. He went around back to the alley to park."

"My goodness, that must have been an awful experience for you this morning at that accident."

"Well, it wasn't pleasant, Mom, but it was very educational. I really had the opportunity to practice hands-on trauma care.

"Oh, by the way, there was this young guy at the accident. His name was Bill and he looked exactly like Dad in that picture in the album at home. You know, the one taken when you and Dad were seniors in college just before you were married. It was really weird because he even had some of the same facial expressions that Dad has."

"Gee, that is surprising, Kathleen. I've always thought Dad was one of a kind."

"I'll stop by Thursday after school and look at that album again if you don't mind, Mom."

"Oh, certainly, in fact why don't you stay for dinner. I'll plan on making your favorite chicken casserole," Lori suggested as she donned her coat and boots.

"Sounds good, Mom. I'll see you about six."

"Oh, Kathleen, my lunch is in the microwave. Why don't you have it and I'll grab a sandwich with Dad at home."

"Perfect, Mom. Thanks."

Lori buttoned her coat and went out the back door to meet Bill and head for home.

10

HEALING TRUTH

Marty nervously stared ahead at the rush-hour traffic on the Los Angeles Freeway. Neither he nor Nancy had spoken a word since leaving the clinic twenty minutes earlier. Nancy continued to wipe an occasional tear from her eye. As they passed the last exit before their turnoff, she suddenly shifted in her seat and looked directly at Marty.

"How did those people know you, Marty?"

Stunned, Marty offered only a slight acknowledgment of Nancy's question with a brief glance in her direction.

Leaning closer to Marty, Nancy persisted. "How did those people know you, Marty?"

Marty dreaded the next few minutes, but

he knew he had to answer. Nancy was a very direct person and would not let the incident drop.

"Nancy, I was hoping you wouldn't ask me that because I will have to expose another person. And just as I am loyal to you and your secret, so I must likewise remain loyal to someone else. If you remember, I was trying to spare you all of this on the way down here when I made an effort to stop you."

"Stop Me? What are you talking about, Marty? This was your idea!"

"Yes, I know Nancy, but on the way down to the clinic I tried to dissuade you because I realized more than ever that the aftereffects would make your life miserable."

"How would you know about the aftereffects?"

Marty struggled to speak. The thought of Nancy's possible reaction to the truth rattled him.

"Well, uh, Nancy. I—"

"Take your time, Marty, I'm listening."

Marty took the off-ramp and headed downtown.

Fifteen minutes later, in the midst of explaining his third child's abortion, he pulled into the parking garage with tears in his eyes.

"I have never been able to forget it. I still have nightmares, and so does Sarah. I thought it would be just another event in my life, but it has become a torture. I try to put it out of my mind and sometimes I'm able to. But eventually it all comes back. I imagine my little child being torn to pieces and I. . . ."

Marty began to weep quietly. Nancy put her hand on his shoulder to comfort him.

"Well, why did you recommend it to me?" she whispered.

"I didn't know what else to say to you. You were so upset and confused."

Marty pulled into the parking space and buried his head in his hands.

"I just can't forget. I can't believe I was so cruel. My poor child."

Marty was overcome with grief, more than ever before. In five years, he had never really faced his child's death, and now, with the additional guilt of suggesting abortion to Nancy, he was beginning to crumble.

"Marty, let's get some fresh air."

Nancy stepped out of the car, walked to Marty's side, and opened the door. As Marty emerged, shaken and embarrassed, Nancy embraced him as she, too, began to weep.

Suddenly, the parking garage began to glow. Surprised, Marty and Nancy looked to the rear of the car from which the light was emanating. There, standing only 3 feet tall, was an angelic-looking little girl with a warm and peaceful smile.

"Hi, Daddy," the girl said. "Don't be afraid. I have come to forgive you."

Looking around for other possible fathers, Marty became confused.

"Little girl, I don't know you. I'm not your daddy."

"Daddy, I forgive you for aborting me five years ago."

Marty clutched Nancy. "What?"

"I forgive you, Daddy. God our Father has sent me to bring you His mercy and love. He wants you to forgive yourself."

The glow began to fade and the little girl's appearance became very real. Nancy was speechless.

"My name is Melissa—the name you and Mommy wanted to give to me if I was a girl."

Melissa approached Marty, but he stepped back in fright.

"Wait a minute! Wait a minute! How do I

know what you say is true?"

"Pick me up, Daddy, and I will show you."

Marty panicked and backed up against the side of the car.

But something was happening to Nancy. She slowly approached Melissa.

"Melissa, did you really come from Heaven?"

"Yes, Nancy, and your little boy is very healthy and wants you to be his mommy."

Nancy put her hands to her mouth, unable to speak. More tears welled up in her eyes.

"A little boy," she thought. "A little boy. Oh, dear God, I almost killed him."

Then, looking at Marty, Nancy insisted, "Marty! Pick up your child."

Marty froze.

Nancy held out her hands, and Melissa walked into her arms. Picking her up, Nancy walked to Marty and held Melissa close to his chest.

"Hold her, Marty. She loves you. She has come a long, long way for this moment."

Trembling, Marty reached out and embraced Melissa, drawing her close to his heart. With her warm little face pressed to his, she whispered, "I love you, Daddy. I forgive you and want you to be at peace."

Marty sobbed and trembled. Nancy reached forward, putting her arms around father and child. Then she prayed, "Thank You, dear God, our Father. I believe. . . . I believe."

"Let's go home, Daddy. I want to see Mommy," Melissa urged.

Marty was speechless as he continued to hug Melissa.

"Marty, why don't you get in the car and I'll drive," Nancy offered as she held the back door open.

En route to Marty's home, Nancy suggested he call ahead. Nodding agreement, Marty flipped open his cell phone and dialed.

"Are you calling Mommy, Daddy?"

"Yes, I am, Melissa, I believe she's home and . . . hello, Sarah? Hi, honey, I'm on the way home and I have a surprise for you. Will you be there for a while? Good. I'll be about another fifteen minutes or so."

Sarah couldn't understand why Marty was coming home so early. It was only 4:30, two hours earlier than his usual arrival time.

"Well, I guess I'll finish trimming the window boxes till Marty arrives," Sarah mused as she picked up her pruning shears and walked to the end of their very large front porch. She and

Marty loved to sit outside in the wicker rocking chairs every evening after dinner.

Halfway through the first window box of Impatiens, she heard Marty's car coming up the driveway. Turning to greet him, she noticed Nancy driving and Marty sitting in the back seat. Sarah hadn't seen Nancy since the company Christmas party two years ago. Sarah didn't attend every year. Confused, she put her shears down and walked down the path to the driveway.

"Hi, Nancy. What a surprise. Is Marty all right?"

"Hello, Sarah. Yes, Marty is fine."

Marty opened the car door as Sarah approached. Stepping out, he reached back in and picked up Melissa. Turning back to face Sarah, he paused, then said, "Honey, I have quite a surprise for you. This is Meli—"

"Hi, Mommy, I'm Melissa."

Complete silence captured the moment. Nancy quickly moved next to Sarah as Marty approached his wife.

"This is Melissa and she has come to bring us peace," Marty said.

"Mommy, I love you."

"I don't understand, Marty, why is this little

girl calling me mommy?"

Nancy stepped closer to Sarah.

"Sarah, Marty probably told you that I was raped in the parking garage a few months ago. Well, as a result I became pregnant. After talking it over with Marty, I decided to have an abortion."

Sarah grew pale and backed several feet away from Nancy.

"Well," Nancy continued, "today was the day for the abortion, but after my experience at the clinic I decided to keep my child and Marty drove me back to the office."

Sarah interrupted, "Marty drove you to the clinic?"

"Yes, but there is more—"

"What's going on Marty, why didn't you tell me about this?"

"Honey, I—"

"Please, Sarah," Nancy interrupted. I must tell you about Melissa."

Melissa quickly wriggled out of Marty's embrace and ran toward Sarah.

"Mommy, I can explain it to you."

Sarah panicked as the vivid memories of her own abortion came rushing back. Holding up her hand, she insisted, "Just a minute, little girl!"

Melissa continued to move closer, reaching out to Sarah.

"Mommy, pick me up."

"Stop," Sarah shouted as she walked back toward the front porch. "Stay away from me little girl; I'm not your mommy. Marty, what is going on here? I want this child and Nancy to leave immediately!"

"No, Mommy! No! I don't want to leave. I came from Heaven to forgive you," Melissa pleaded as she ran to Sarah.

"Get away! Get away!" Sarah yelled as she bolted up the stairs to the front door.

Melissa ran to the bottom of the stairs and whispered, "But Mommy, I love you. I want to be with you. I forgive you for aborting me. I—"

"Stop! Stop! Stop!" Sarah screamed as she held her hands to her ears and ran inside, slamming the door.

Stunned, Marty ran up the stairs and tried to open the door, but it was locked.

"Sarah, please let me in, I have to explain this to you."

"No! No! No! Go away! Go away!" Sarah screamed as she ran up the stairs to the bedroom.

"Marty!" Nancy called.

Marty spun around to see Melissa crying. He picked her up and held her close to his chest as she sobbed.

"Melissa, don't cry, I will convince Mommy to come back out and see you.

Struggling to compose herself, Melissa sobbed, "No Daddy. She won't come back out. Mommy has rejected me. If she had accepted me and God's mercy and forgiveness, I would have been able to stay for a few days. But because she has refused, I will have to go back, and that means. . . " Melissa lost her voice for a moment, then continued... "that means I will have to go back without Mommy wanting me a . . . a second time." Melissa burst into sobs and threw her arms around Marty's neck. She clung to him, trembling.

Nancy was overcome. Sitting on the front porch steps, she silently prayed, "Dear God, please help this poor child. She is crushed." Suddenly, a Heavenly silence covered the earth. A soft and gentle light approached the porch and completely absorbed Melissa. Marty and Nancy stood in awe as Melissa was lifted from Marty's arms and slowly transported up into the sky and beyond the clouds.

As she reached the upper atmosphere,

the light began to fade, revealing her guardian angel, who was holding her in his arms and racing her Heavenward. In seconds, they were approaching the staging area above the earth where 2 million souls were still praying.

Spontaneously, from all directions, hundreds of souls began to return from earth. Many were smiling and filled with joy. Others were profoundly sad and crying. All immediately knelt and prayed to their Father. An equal number of guardians knelt beside them. Their prayer was one of praise and thanksgiving for the opportunity to see their mothers and fathers and bring them God's love.

Overwhelmed, Marty sat on the front porch steps and buried his head in his hands. Still weeping and confused, he was finally experiencing his long-delayed grief.

Nancy slowly walked up the stairs and patted him on the shoulder.

"I'll take your car home for tonight, Marty."

Marty tried to respond but lost his voice. Overwhelmed herself, Nancy slowly made her way down the stairs and walked to the car. As she opened the door, she stopped, looked back, and quietly assured Marty, "We'll talk in the morning."

11

DISBELIEF

Arthur Strickland sat motionless in his hospital bed. He had been staring out the window of his private room for hours. The morning rain had stopped during his lunch, most of which sat uneaten on his night stand. Arthur usually had a healthy appetite, but after the accident four days earlier, he had been placed in a full body cast, which hampered his usual behaviors. As a physician of thirty-five years, he knew that he would heal in time and that his appetite and mobility would return. But despite his knowledge of the better days ahead, he remained somber and exceedingly pensive.

As he gazed at the early spring clouds rolling by, his mind repeatedly played back his medical

career as if some unknown force was rewinding a
tape over and over again. Why couldn't he shift
to another subject? Why did the tape always start
at medical school graduation? He had been a
diligent, energetic student who looked forward
to taking part in the healing profession. He vividly
remembered standing at the podium and
receiving his diploma from the dean of
students, Dr. Albert Fisher, whom he admired for
his vast knowledge and experience. Sitting in the
front row was his former fiancee, Marsha Linn,
who had left him for a fellow classmate and was
now seven months pregnant. Arthur loved
Marsha dearly and had always treated her with
great respect. Deep in his heart, he had always
felt that if she hadn't become pregnant and felt
compelled to marry the father, she eventually
would have come back to him and would have
become his wife. The hurt had never really left
him, even though he had been happily married to
his wife, Connie, for more than fifteen years
before their very sad and unexpected divorce.
Now, as he replayed his life again and again, he
became depressed at his losses.

"First Marsha to a classmate and then
Connie because of my profession," he thought.
"If I was a neurologist, I suppose Connie would

have accepted that. But because I'm an abortionist, she said she couldn't live with me. She never really told me why she objected to my being an abortionist. All she said was that it was not something a doctor should be doing. I tried to explain to her that state law requires that abortions may only be performed by medical doctors, but she wouldn't listen. And now, for the past fifteen years, I've lived without my wife."

Arthur had performed more than sixty thousand abortions, and despite his frequent nightmares, he regarded himself as one of the best in the business. He even performed very late-term abortions. Several in recent years had been up to eight months. Although he defended his participation in America's scandal, he frequently suffered the pain of guilt and knew he needed to make a change.

As he pushed the button to adjust his bed to a more vertical position, the phone rang.

"Hello."

"Dad. Hi."

"Susan, sweetheart. Where are you?"

Arthur's daughter, Susan, and son, Arthur Jr., had stopped in to visit several times in the past three days, but both had returned to college

when spring break came to an end the previous
 day.

"I'm back at school, Dad. I just wanted to let
you know that I made it safe and sound and that
the weather is great. How are you doing?"

"About the same as yesterday. I can't talk
much above a whisper because of the pain, and I
don't have any appetite to speak of, but I'm told I
will be going home in about a week. So that is
encouraging."

"Dad, when you're ready to go back to
work, I think it would be a good idea if you
specialized in something else."

"Why, honey? I enjoy being an OB/Gyn."

"That part is Ok, Dad, but don't you do
abortions, too?"

Arthur was speechless. How did she know?
He and Connie had always discussed it in private.

"Well, I have done a few, but only in rare
circumstances."

"I remember you and Mom arguing about it
fifteen years ago, just before you were divorced."

"Uh, well, ok Susan, I will give that some
thought."

"Great, Dad. Well, I better get off the

phone. Long distance and I'm on a budget. Love you. Bye."

"Bye–bye, sweetheart. I love you, too."

Arthur hung up the phone and tried to take a deep breath. The shock of his daughter knowing his secret unnerved him.

"I don't believe this," he thought. "Some people make such a fuss about nothing. This is a legal medical procedure. What's the big deal?"

The partly sunny day was becoming more overcast again. Arthur settled back and gazed at the changing sky. As his mind returned to his conversation with Susan, he thought he saw something pass by his window. Thinking it to be a bird, he pondered the species.

"Robin, maybe. It's early spring."

Then another and another "something" passed by his window. They were much larger than birds, but they were moving too fast to recognize.

"Maybe it's just dust or leaves in this early spring wind," Arthur guessed as he continued to stare into the heavens.

Gradually, the sky grew very dark as rain clouds approached the hospital. A light drizzle began to pelt the window panes. Suddenly, a flash of light lit up the entire parking lot below, and Arthur began to count seconds, waiting for the thunder. But none ensued. Then, in a quiet moment, a light appeared at the foot of his bed. He could see nothing but a gentle, warm glow. The light moved slowly toward the window and then outside the window, where it descended gradually toward the parking lot below. Alarmed, Arthur reached for his buzzer to call the hospital nurse and pushed it continuously.

"Nurse! Nurse! There is a light in my room."

A staff nurse and an orderly came running to the room and stopped at the door.

"What is the matter, Dr. Strickland?"

"There was a light at the end of my bed. It just moved through the window and down into the parking lot."

"We don't see any light," the orderly responded.

"But it is right there in the parking lot. Take a look."

The nurse walked to the window and peered down into the parking lot.

"All I see is cars, Dr. Strickland. Have you taken your nap today? Possibly you're hallucinating from your pain medication."

"Hallucinating?" Arthur bellowed. "No I'm not hallucinating. Can't you see that bright light in the parking lot?

"No, doctor, but I will have your physician give you a different prescription."

"I don't need another prescription. I need someone who can see clearly!"

As the nurse and orderly left the room, the warm glow again appeared at the foot of Arthur's bed. Suddenly, a little boy materialized and looked directly at him. He smiled innocently and said, "I have come to forgive you for aborting me, Dr. Strickland. I have come to tell you that God loves you and wants to save you."

Arthur was jolted from his anger as fear consumed him. He tried to push himself farther back in his bed, but two teenagers suddenly appeared and began to wheel his bed toward the window.

One, a tall boy, cranked the head of the bed up as high as possible, while the other, a saintly looking girl, instructed Arthur to look down into the parking lot twenty feet below.

"No!" Arthur shouted. "No! I'm not looking at anything. Leave me alone!"

"Look, doctor. Look at the souls who have come to visit you," the girl encouraged.

Arthur began to panic and shake. Pain shot through his chest as the sutures from his operation pulled tight from his trembling.

"Your life was spared in the accident," the little boy declared. "That snowplow was pushed aside by two of the children you aborted. One more split second and it would have crushed you completely."

Arthur gasped for air as he trembled in fear. His life of butchery was racing before his eyes. He could see the clinic. He could see the years, the dates, the numbers.

"Look! Look at the souls who have come to visit you and pray for you," the little boy insisted.

"No! No!" Arthur screamed as he threw his hands up to his face and covered his eyes. "Make them go away! Make them go away!"

Immediately the little boy climbed up into the bed and pulled Arthur's hands away from his eyes. "Look" he ordered. "They love you! Look at them!"

Slowly the abortionist opened his eyes and gasped in shock. He could see more than sixty thousand children and young adults looking directly at him. They were human and they were alive. They completely covered the hospital grounds. In an instant, he could see everyone individually and collectively. He was given to know each one intimately, and realized their complete suffering at the moments of their deaths. But he also felt their great love and forgiveness without a word spoken. Each child, regardless of age, was beautiful. All pleaded with their eyes for his acceptance.

Suddenly, however, the abortionist pushed away from the window. His heart was racing and his breathing was labored. "Put my bed back where it belongs and get out of here" he ordered. "I don't want your forgiveness! I want to be left alone!"

"Doctor, if you don't accept our Father's mercy, you could be in danger of losing your soul for eternity," the little boy pleaded.

"I don't want to hear that! Go tell it to someone else!"

The little boy again stepped closer to Arthur.

"Doctor, please accept my forgiveness."

"No! Strickland bellowed," Get out of here! Leave me alone! Leave me alone!!"

Suddenly, loud footsteps could be heard running toward the doctor's room. And just as suddenly as they had appeared, the children disappeared amid Arthur's continued and boisterous objections

12

UNEXPECTED VISITORS

Kathleen turned the night security lights on and stepped out of the front door to her apartment. After setting the alarm she locked the dead bolt and walked to her car. With another hour of daylight left, it would be an easy ride home to Mom and Dad's for dinner. The weather bureau had forecast rain but so far the sun was still shining.

Twelve miles away, Bill had just finished setting the dinner table as Lori emerged from the kitchen with the hot chicken casserole and placed it in the middle of the tablecloth.

"Umm, boy, that smells good, Lori," Bill remarked as he lifted the lid for a look at Kathleen's favorite dish.

"Patience, honey. Kathleen will be here in a few minutes."

"Just looking," Bill smiled as he replaced the lid.

Standing at the kitchen sink, Lori could see through the window and down the block about a quarter-mile. Suddenly, around the turn, she noticed Kathleen approaching in her Toyota.

"Here she comes, honey."

"Great! I'm starved," Bill shouted as he opened the door and walked outside to greet Kathleen.

Lori remembered Kathleen speaking about the young man at the accident.

"I think I'll run into the den and get the album before dinner," she murmured to herself. "Kathleen mentioned she wanted to look at it."

As Kathleen entered the foyer, Lori walked into the living room with the album and plopped it on the sofa.

"Hi, Kathleen. Here's the album you wanted to see. I'll be in the kitchen for a few minutes. Help yourself."

"Thanks, Mom."

Kathleen sat down and began to thumb through the 25-year-old album.

"Wow, Dad. I had forgotten about all these

pictures of you and Mom. This one of Mom looks a little bit like me, but not enough to tell that she is my mom. Here's one of you, Dad, and. . . oh, here is the one of you and Mom at college. Gee, you look exactly like that guy at the accident this morning. Gosh, it's amazing, Dad, you really look exactly like him. It's creepy."

Bill wandered over to the couch and sat down next to Kathleen.

"Which one, honey?"

"Here, where you and Mom are standing in front of NYU."

"So this guy looked exactly like me in this picture? I guess I was about 21 at that time."

"Yes, he did, Dad, and I mean he looked *exactly* like you."

"Let's see," Lori interrupted as she emerged from the kitchen.

"This picture here, Mom. See Dad's expression? It's identical to that guy's this morning."

"Did you speak with him?" Lori asked.

"No, but I did hear his voice and it was much younger than Dad's, so I wouldn't be able to compare it with Dad's voice now."

"Oh, of course not. And why would it even be the same anyway?" Lori concluded.

Bill was silent. A pensive look came over his face.

"Well, let's eat and we can talk about it," Lori ordered as she headed for the kitchen.

As Bill and Kathleen took their seats, Lori set the vegetables on the table and sat down.

"I'll say grace," Kathleen suggested, and everyone bowed their heads.

"Dear God, our Father, in Jesus' name we thank You for all of Your blessings, especially this wonderful meal we have before us. Please help others who are less fortunate to have sufficient food through the generosity of us, their brothers and sisters. And please help the man who was in that horrible accident this morning to recover completely. Thank You. Amen."

Bill and Lori echoed an "Amen" as Kathleen passed the casserole to Lori. Suddenly, the doorbell chimed, surprising everyone.

"Who could that possibly be just before dark " Bill asked as he pushed his chair back and walked to the front door.

Lori and Kathleen heard the door open, but no one spoke. Silent moments passed. Gradually, Lori rose from her chair and walked slowly toward the foyer. Kathleen followed. As Lori walked up behind Bill, she could see two people standing outside the door in the fading light. Bill was attempting to speak with them, but he couldn't seem to utter the words.

"Who is it, honey?" Lori asked, her voice barely above a whisper.

As she walked closer to the door, she could see a young man and a younger woman standing beside him.

"May I help you?" she started to say, but suddenly she threw her hands up to her face and whispered, "Oh, dear God, dear God." She grabbed Bill's arm for support as she started to lose her balance.

"Mom!" Kathleen blurted as she raced forward and supported Lori. "What is the matter? Who are these people? I . . . oh, it's you Bill. I saw you this morning and you look just like Dad and...Dad, this is the guy I saw this mor...Dad, what is the matter?"

Tears were streaming down Bill's face as Lori hung onto him with her face buried in his shoulder.

"Who are you? Who are you?" Lori demanded as she began to lose control and sob.

Kathleen was shaken and confused.

"What's going on, Dad?" she asked.

Suddenly the young woman stepped in

front of the door.

"Kathleen, I'm Maria. I was there this morning also. Do you remember me?"

"Yes. Yes, I do remember you, and . . . Oh! You look just like Mom's picture with Dad and...-"

Kathleen was becoming frightened.

"Mom! Dad! Please tell me what is going on!!"

Maria stepped closer and put her hand on Kathleen's shoulder. Gently she whispered, "I'm your sister."

Lori crumpled to the floor, and Bill knelt down and embraced her.

"Dear God, Have mercy on us," Bill sobbed as he hugged Lori. Both were trembling and sobbing.

Tears were welling up in Kathleen's eyes, but she fought to retain her composure.

"And Bill...Bill...Are you my brother?"

"Yes, Kathleen. I am your brother. Mom and Dad have never seen us before, but we have come to help them."

"Never seen you before? Do you mean they gave you up for adoption? And what do you mean 'help them'?"

"Please! Please! Leave us alone. Go away. Leave us alone!" Bill sobbed as he held his trembling wife.

Immediately Maria reached forward and touched Bill and Lori, who became completely limp. Then she gently placed her hand on Kathleen's head and said, "Peace."
Kathleen immediately felt dazed. Maria slowly walked her to the living room and sat her down. Bill helped his now-serene mother and father to their feet and escorted them to the large couch next to Kathleen. Once all were seated, silence ensued. After a few moments, however, Bill Jr. moved his chair closer, looked his mother and father lovingly in the eye, and spoke with a peaceful and gentle voice.

"Mom! Dad! We have come from Heaven to bring you God's love and mercy. We have come to forgive you . . . to help you heal. Please, just listen, and then decide for yourselves."

13

MAJOR BATTLE

High above the earth, millions of returning souls rapidly filled the staging area. The joy of most was unmistakable, as the victory of love glowed from their beautiful faces. Not all had enjoyed victory, however, and Carrie sadly received them one by one. Those who decided they did not want to try again quietly moved to the area set aside for the return trip home. Those who were determined to try again, in spite of their heartbreak, moved to a separate area, where those who had failed before them were gathered.

Carrie spoke: "My brothers and sisters. Eleven million were rejected. Nine million of you have chosen to return. As you wait and suffer, your prayers are urgently needed for those of us who are about to embark. We are the last to journey to earth. There are almost 2 million of us, and we are all going to the same place. Fifty percent of all the children Father sends to this city are killed in abortion. The atmosphere will be extremely hostile. Abortion is firmly entrenched in this evil place. You are those with the strongest spirits. Your prayers are most powerful. In spite of defeat, you have chosen to return to the pain and hurt in order to save your mothers and fathers. Those who will journey with me today have become weary and anxious as they have seen so many return without victory. You must be their champions of prayer to keep them determined. They have human spirits now and can become discouraged very quickly. Please pray continuously. Jesus will be your strength."

Carrie moved to the massive assembly area, where those who had succeeded and those who had failed but did not wish to return to earth had gathered for the return trip home.

"My brothers and sisters. We are about to depart. Our destination is the worst abortion center in America. Many perils await us. You are 29 million strong. Please stay vigilant in prayer. We have not failed because so many have returned without success. Rather, we have been victorious because 27 million hearts and souls have been saved."

Carrie seemed exhausted as she walked to the center of the staging area. She had spent the last five days and nights in prayer with her 2 million comrades. The intensity with which they had prayed had strengthened her spiritually, but in her human condition it had physically drained her. Now she was facing the challenge for which she had come—to save her mother's soul. Unlike many who had experienced abortion and later repented and sought salvation, her mother remained adamant about her so-called right to "choose." Carrie knew this would be a very difficult battle, but she was prepared to fight. Gradually she moved closer to the edge of earth's atmosphere. Then she turned and faced her fellow pilgrims.

"Children of abortion! Children of the culture of death! Children of God who created you! It is time to return to the place of our beginning. It is time to meet the challenge set before us. It is time to fight as we have never fought before. Our weapon is love. Limitless love. Faithful love. Love for those whom we wish to save and love for all those who hinder us. It is our love that will destroy the evil that battles against our victory. Brothers and sisters, raise your hands to our Father."

As 4 million children and guardian angels raised their hands in prayer, Carrie began to pray.

"Dear loving Father, we go now in union with your Holy Spirit to save millions of souls. Be our strength. Our courage. Our determination. Our perseverance. In Jesus' name we ask for victory."

Carrie moved to the very edge of the atmosphere.

"Step forward, my brothers and sisters. Prepare yourselves for battle!"

Two million ready solders of love moved to Carrie's side.

"All you angels and Saints, pray before the throne of our loving Father for our success."

Suddenly, the universe exploded in a flash of blinding light as 2 million souls shot to earth like so many bolts of lightning. Directly ahead of them was the most dangerous place in America for a child in the womb—New York City.

14

CONVERSION

Two hours had passed since Maria had helped her dazed sister Kathleen to a seat and Bill had escorted his devastated mother and father to the couch. Maria had told most of the story while Kathleen remained silent and motionless. Bill and Lori had intermittently sobbed and hugged each other as the tragedy unfolded.

"Mom and Dad," Bill continued, "the bottom line is this: Father wills for you to be forever with Him in heaven. His mercy will bring you there if you repent of aborting Maria and me and humbly seek and accept His forgiveness."

Neither Bill nor Lori responded. They remained stone-faced and silent, stunned by the return of their children.

"Mom, Dad," Kathleen interrupted, "I want to think this is all a dream, but we all know better. I know it is excruciatingly painful to see your children who you rejected so many years ago. And I am sure it is immensely difficult to forgive yourselves. But please know that I forgive you. After all, you brought me into the world and gave me life. That was twenty-three years ago and you have changed. Besides, God has forgiven you. You must forgive yourselves."

"But Kathleen, honey, we actually—" Bill began, but Lori put her hand to his mouth.

"Enough!" she said. "We have spent two hours speaking of this and now we are just going to repeat ourselves." Then, turning to Bill, she said, "I forgive you, honey, and I hope you will forgive me."

Then she knelt down next to the couch and prayed, "Dear Father in heaven, I repent of having killed my children, and I seek Your mercy and forgiveness."

Bill was deeply moved to hear his wife praying again after almost thirty years. Since the abortions, she had ceased practicing as a Catholic and rarely even mentioned God's name. Now Bill knew that it was his turn to return to his spiritual roots, proclaim his guilt, and seek God's mercy.

He knelt next to his wife. "Dear Lord Jesus," he prayed. "Thank You for saving us by Your cross of suffering. I confess my sins to You and seek Your forgiveness. I will return to Your church and sacraments, and will never stray again."

Immediately Bill and Maria glowed with a magnificent brilliance as tears of great joy and victory streamed down their faces.

"Mom and Dad," Maria began, "this is a joyful moment for Almighty God our Father. He has heard your prayer of repentance, and now He wants you to help Him save the abortionist who ended our lives. He was in a terrible accident this morning, but Kathleen saved his life. She didn't know who he was or who we were, but she saved the life of the man who killed her brother and sister. Now, Father is asking all of us to help save this man who could be in danger of losing his soul."

Kathleen was speechless. So much was unfolding so quickly she could barely process it.

Bill stood and faced his mother, father, and sisters.

"We must go to the hospital immediately. Dr. Strickland has already rejected God's mercy.

All of our brothers and sisters who were aborted by him are praying for his salvation at this moment. They are all there at the hospital, more than sixty thousand of them. We need your help."

Lori began to shiver. "I can't. . . . I can't go near that man again," she said. "I don't want to see him." Tears welled up in her eyes as Bill put his arm around her.

"Mom," Maria pleaded, "your prayers for the abortionist who killed your children will be extremely powerful. You will be choosing mercy over vengeance. Your prayers and Dad's prayers can change Dr. Strickland's heart."

"Give us a moment," Bill requested as he slowly walked Lori to the kitchen.

Maria, Bill, and Kathleen huddled in prayer by the front door, hoping to change Lori's mind.

Lori said, "But, honey, what if he recognizes us and what if he tells—"

"Don't worry, honey, he will never recognize us after all these years," Bill assured. "And besides, we are talking about his soul. It's possible he could be lost for eternity."

"Yes. . . . Yes, he could," Lori agreed as she stood up and faced Bill. "Ok. For the sake of his soul, I will go. I just hope he doesn't remember.

There has already been enough hurt."

The early-evening traffic moved rapidly toward downtown Albany. The rush hour traffic had subsided and the Sullivan's with their three children made excellent time, pulling into the main parking lot of the hospital just before 8:30 p.m.

"We'd better get inside fast, Dad and Mom. Visiting hours are over in thirty minutes," Maria warned.

"I've got the jitters, honey," Lori whispered to Bill as they shut the car door and headed for the lobby.

Inside, Kathleen approached the information desk and asked for Arthur's room.

"Arthur Strickland?" the candy striper said. "Yes, ma'am, he is in 314 on the south side."

"Let's go, everyone," Maria suggested. "The elevators are over here."

Arthur was just settling back into his pillow after enjoying his first full dinner since his operation. The evening staff members were not familiar with his early afternoon encounter with the children and were attending to other patients as the Sullivan's walked into his room. Kathleen approached him first.

"How are you, Dr. Strickland?" she asked.

Surprised, Arthur tried to sit up a bit.

"Uh . . . well, I'm doing a little bit better now that I've had some food," he replied. Then, looking more intensely at Kathleen, he asked,

"Aren't you the nice lady who helped me in the ambulance?"

Surprised that he recognized her, Kathleen responded, "Yes, I am, doctor."

"Oh, thank you so much. What is your name?"

"Kathleen Sullivan."

"Well, Kathleen, you saved my life. How can I thank you? You were the only one who stepped forward. I'm a physician, and I know that I had only another minute or two before I would have bled to death."

"Yes, that is true, doctor," Bill Jr. said as he stepped forward. "You were very close to death."

"Who are you?" Arthur asked in a somewhat annoyed fashion.

"I'm Bill Sullivan, Jr. This is my mother, Lori Sullivan, and my dad, Bill Sullivan, and my sister, Maria Sullivan."

"Well, you must be very proud of your daughter, Mr. and Mrs. Sullivan. I remember her telling the ambulance personnel that she is a medical student in her final year."

"Yes, we are proud of her, Dr. Strickland," Bill Sr. responded.

Maria stepped forward. "Dr. Strickland," she said, "my brother Bill and I have come to forgive you."

Arthur grew pale and silent, then whispered, "What do you mean 'forgive' me?"

Lori stepped behind her husband, trying to hide her face.

"We have come to forgive you for killing us in abortion."

Fear gripped Arthur. This was the second time today he had been confronted with the horror of his past. He began to tremble once again.

Kathleen stepped forward and, as she had done in the ambulance, made the sign of the cross on Arthur's forehead. He grew unusually silent amid his fear. He had a trust in Kathleen that he had never experienced in another human being.

"They have come to forgive you, doctor," Kathleen said. "They have come from Heaven."

Arthur covered his mouth with his hand.

"Doctor," Bill Jr. said, "God our Father loves you and wants to save your soul for all eternity. He has a place for you in Heaven."

"Heaven?" Arthur bellowed. "How can an abortionist go to Heaven? There will be sixty thousand human beings waiting to accuse me when I die."

"No. That isn't true," Maria pleaded. "Those children love you and have been praying for you for years. Bill and I are just two, but the rest are outside right now in the parking lot pleading with God your Father for your salvation. They are praying you will repent and accept His forgiveness."

"Forgiveness?" Arthur argued. "How can I be forgiven? I can't bring sixty thousand human beings back to life."

"God our Father has already forgiven you through His son Jesus Christ. He is God the Son and is waiting for you to repent and accept His forgiveness and mercy."

"Please," Bill pleaded. "We have come a long way to save you. Listen to God's Spirit speaking to you. He speaks through us."

"I'm too far gone," Arthur argued. "Too many years. Too many murders. Why should I be forgiven?"

"Because God loves you. You are his child . He created you," Maria cried.

"No!! . . . I don't believe you. Go away...leave me alone!"
Suddenly, Maria knelt down next to Strickland's bed and covering her face with her hands began to weep.

"Stop! Please stop! Don't hurt my child again," Lori pleaded. "You have already hurt her enough. Repent and accept God's forgiveness. We did, and we have been liberated from the horrible guilt and shame."

The glow from the parking lot began again, growing brighter and brighter as Arthur's stubbornness continued.

"Look," Bill Jr. cried, "all of your victims are praying for you. They love you and want you with them in paradise for eternity."

Sixty thousand souls began to chant in beautiful unison, praying for their abortionist to change his heart. The parking lot grew brighter from the power of prayer as time was running out.

"Hurry and repent, Dr. Strickland," Maria pleaded. "We are being called back. Please accept God's mercy."

"Dad! Mom!" Kathleen cried. "Kneel down. Quickly! We have free will to pray or not to pray. Our prayers will be very powerful."

"Dear Jesus," Kathleen began. "Please save Dr. Strickland. He needs so much help so quickly. We forgive him and pray for his salvation. Please deliver him from the evil that grips his soul."

"Yes Dear Jesus. Save him!" Lori cried.

"God our father. Please save our brother Arthur," Bill Sr. Pleaded.

Suddenly, tears began to stream from Arthur's eyes.

Kathleen leapt to her feet, put her head on his chest, and hugged him. "It's Ok, it's Ok . . . go ahead and cry. Jesus loves you. It's Ok to accept His mercy."

"I do . . . I do repent. . . ," Arthur cried out as he wept and shook in pain. "I do accept. Please forgive . . . forgive me, dear God."

Suddenly, Maria's and Bill's faces glowed with their Heavenly beauty as the abortionist repented and accepted God's mercy. Meanwhile, the parking lot below grew as bright as day as the multitudes rejoiced in a prayer of thanksgiving for the great mercy of Almighty God. In the next instant, sixty thousand souls singing magnificent hymns of praise shot heavenward in a blinding flash of victorious light.

As Kathleen reassured Arthur, he wiped a

flood of joyful tears from his eyes.

"I never thought I could be so relieved and peaceful," he offered as he surveyed the family who had brought God's salvation to his soul. "Mrs. Sullivan, I do remember you and your husband now. I do remember you. It has been so many years. You know, I never really wanted to do abortions. We call them terminations, but that is just a word we use to camouflage the killing. Every time I took the life of another tiny child I was trying to undo what happened to me in medical school. My fiancée left me for another student and became pregnant. I always felt that if it wasn't for the pregnancy, she would have come back to me. Somehow, in my confused thinking and pain, I hoped to eliminate children in the womb and regain the happiness I lost when Marsha left me because of her child. It's illogical, I know. Maybe some of it was vengeance. I'm not sure, but it's over now. I will never do another abortion as long as I live."

All five family members remained silent as they listened to the man who had killed two of them and whose life had been saved by three of them.

Suddenly, Arthur became silent. Staring at each one and then pensively at Kathleen, he asked, "Mrs. Sullivan, I remember a pro-life sidewalk counselor saving one of your children from abortion even though I came outside to try to convince you otherwise. How many children did you ultimately have?"

Lori panicked. Her voice failed as she tried to speak. Grasping Bill's arm for support, she buried her head in his shoulder. Tense moments passed as Bill put his arm around Lori.

"Three, Dr. Strickland," he reluctantly whispered as Lori began to weep.

"Three," Kathleen repeated to herself. "How could it be three?" She turned to her mother and father. "Dad, Mom...what do you mean three? I mean, there are only three of us anyway."

Arthur put his hand to his mouth, realizing he had made a terrible mistake.

"Do you mean . . .," Kathleen continued, "Do you mean . . . No! No! Oh, No, Dear Lord," she blurted out as she began to tremble and weep.

"Do you mean you were going to abort me also? Mom . . . Were you going to kill me, too? Just like Bill and Maria . . . Were you going to kill me, too? No! No! I can't take any more of this. . . . Dear Jesus, help me, please help me," she pleaded as she turned to the abortionist who had intended to take her life.

Hysterically she screamed, you were going to kill me...and I saved your life..."

Sobbing and hysterical, Kathleen burst from the room and ran down the hallway to the elevators.

Arthur Strickland buried his face in his hands and groaned in remorse as he once again suffered the pain of hurting innocent people.

15

DEVOTED LOVE

Kathleen steered her Toyota
Corolla into the parking lot of All Saints Catholic
Church in downtown Albany. Directly ahead of
her was the side entrance, which she had used
for many years. When she was a child, her mother
and father had used the main entrance, but once
she had made her First Holy Communion, Bill and
Lori had rarely attended Sunday Mass. For the
next ten years, Kathleen had ridden to Sunday
Mass with her cousins, who lived two doors
away. She loved her Catholic faith, and once she
was able to afford her own car, she had begun
attending daily Mass at 6:30 a.m. Immediately
afterward, she would spend time with Jesus in
the Blessed Sacrament before heading to her first

class at New York University. Now, seven years later, as she was preparing to graduate from medical school, Kathleen found herself returning to the source of her peace and joy.

Slowly she emerged from her car and began the short walk to the church. Usually full of life and with a bounce in her step, today Kathleen could muster no more than a slow and tired pace. Her innocent Irish face was somber and sad as she turned the handle and opened the door to her earthly Heaven. Quietly she moved to the center of the main aisle and walked to the second pew from the altar. There, directly in front of her, was the peace and joy she was unable to find elsewhere. She genuflected, entered the pew, and knelt. In silence she looked directly at the beautiful gold tabernacle and closed her eyes.

A few moments passed before she opened her eyes and audibly said, "Jesus. . . Dear Lord. . . I'm so sorry. I just couldn't take anymore. I felt so unwanted. So unloved. I . . ."

Tears began to form in Kathleen's eyes as she struggled to continue.

"I couldn't believe someone tried to kill me. He tried to convince Mom to kill me. And he had already killed Maria and Bill. I. . . ."

Kathleen put her hands to her face and burst into tears. Although the church was large, her weeping could be heard throughout the turn-of-the-century edifice.

"Please, Dear Lord Jesus . . . forgive me," she cried as she sat down and agonized over her burst of rage toward Arthur Strickland. "Mom was going to . . . Mom was going to kill me. And I don't know if she even . . . loves . . . loves me," Kathleen sobbed as she trembled without relief. "I don't know if Dad loves me, either. He . . . he was going to kill me, too. Jesus, help me . . . please . . ."

Kathleen slumped in the pew and wept. She couldn't stop shaking.

As her tears and trembling continued, a beautiful and soft light consumed her. Instantly she looked to the tabernacle. Then she heard a gentle and kind voice.

"Be peaceful, My child, I have heard you. Your suffering has been put to good use. Dr. Strickland has been converted. His heart and soul will grow in love. But child, you must trust in My love for *you*. I know your heart even when you do not. Your heart has always been with Me as you have willed it to be. Your human emotions are not sins. They are an indication of your pain. You have offered your suffering to Me over and over again for many years. I use your offerings for much good. Many souls have turned back to Me because of your sacrifices. Do not judge yourself. I know of your love for Me. It is a true love, a love not based on My gifts but a love that loves Me for who I am. You bring much joy to My heart. Continue in My love and be not afraid. I love you and am with you always."

Kathleen sat motionless and silent. Complete peace consumed her. Her tears and trembling subsided. Her peace and joy were restored. Jesus had spoken, and nothing else was necessary. Her soul had been fed. Her heart had been healed.

"Thank You," she whispered. "Thank You for loving me. Thank You for being here. You are always here. You always love. You always forgive. You always heal. I love you, Dear Jesus."

Kathleen's face was radiant. Her smile was filled with great peace and joy. Only the souls in heaven would recognize and understand her beautiful reflection of divine grace.

She waited patiently for a reply from her Lord—but none came forth. As a true soldier of Christ, she understood the silence. She knew that God ventures into time for the perception of His suffering children in their moments of great need. And now, with renewed assurance of her place in her Savior's heart, she realized her great need had been filled. She also knew she must continue in the "Valley of Tears" and finish her pilgrimage to her Father in Heaven, as all souls must. She was no exception.

Kathleen bowed her head and prayed once more.

"Dear God, our Father, thank You for saving Dr. Strickland. Please bring healing to his suffering heart and memory. I ask that You send many holy souls to be part of his life to encourage and support him. And please help him to persevere in Your grace."

Kathleen paused for a few moments as she looked lovingly at her Lord in the tabernacle. Then she whispered, "I must return, Lord—return and seek forgiveness from Dr. Strickland."

She rose, genuflected, and walked to the side entrance. The man she had saved from earthly and spiritual death needed to heal from the past even more than she. Her apology would speed the process immeasurably. Arthur's hospital room was only three miles away. Kathleen would be there in ten minutes.

16

DISCOURAGEMENT

Carrie pulled a tissue from her purse and dusted off her shoes. She had landed in Central Park, in the heart of New York City, and had walked about a half-mile before emerging on the Upper West Side. Sitting on a park bench, she surveyed the neighborhood. Neat and well-maintained apartment buildings lined the street. Uniformed doormen could be seen in front of many of the residences, opening and closing doors of expensive European and American automobiles as they arrived and departed. The residents appeared to be international, middle-aged, professional, well–dressed, and very wealthy.

"So this is where I was conceived thirty-three years ago," Carrie pondered as she settled back on the wooden bench. "And Mom still lives here."

Carrie's mother, Loretta Brown, worked for the United Nations in Manhattan and was two days from retirement. She had been a Spanish translator since graduating from college. Both her mother and father had emigrated from Puerto Rico and spoke Spanish exclusively in their home. Loretta had learned most of her English in grammar school. Now, after forty-three years of faithful service to the United Nations, she was ready to join the ranks of the retired and reap some of the rewards.

Loretta's abortion at age 32 was only a faint memory. And her four-year relationship with a young co-worker, who had departed upon her announcement that he was a father, was all but forgotten.

Patiently waiting outside Loretta's apartment building, Carrie pondered her strategy—especially the method she would employ to introduce herself.

"I can't approach her as she exits the elevator because I won't be able to get into the building. If I approach her as she walks outside, she might just think I'm a street beggar.

Maybe I should give a note to the doorman to deliver to her."

Twenty minutes later, as the uniformed, sixty-something doorman paced up and down under the awning, Carrie casually strolled up and handed him a note for her mother.

"Hi, I'm Carrie Brown," she said. "Could you pass this on to my Mom, Loretta Brown, when you see her this morning?"

"Oh, certainly. I'll be happy to," the smiling professional replied.

"Thank you very much. Just tell her I'll contact her later."

"Will do," he replied as he placed the note in his coat pocket.

Carrie walked to the end of the block and crossed the street. Looking back to make sure the doorman wasn't watching, she stepped into a coffee shop and took a table next to the window. Unsure of the time her mother went to work, Carrie had to keep looking directly at the entrance to the building.

Twenty minutes later, at 8:15, her vigilance paid off. As Loretta exited the building, the doorman approached and handed her the note. She nodded, took the note, and walked slowly toward the corner, where a friend of twenty-six years would pick her up and drive her to the U.N.

Moments later, while reading the note, she stopped, looked back at the doorman, and cautiously proceeded to the corner. Just before reaching the spot where she would meet her friend, she put the note in her pocket and pulled out a tissue. Turning away from the doorman, she began to wipe tears from her eyes.

"Now," Carrie cried as she bolted from the coffee shop and charged across the street to meet her mother.

Carrie jumped over the curb and walked right up to her mother. Startled, Loretta stepped back.

"Mom, I'm Carrie, your daughter. Don't be afraid. I have come from Heaven to bring you God's love."

"I beg your pardon, young lady. I do not have a daughter."

"Mom, I forgive you for aborting me. And I have come to tell you that God's mercy is yours if you will only repent. He loves you. And I love you."

Loretta, a tall and sophisticated woman, backed up even farther.

"You are very mistaken, young lady. Now leave me alone or I will call the doorman."

Beep! Beep! A gray sedan interrupted as Vicki Rodriguez rolled down the window. "Hop in, Loretta, I have cars behind me," she called.

Loretta opened the door and stepped inside as Carrie stared in disbelief, stunned by her mother's complete rejection.

As the sedan sped off, Vicki rolled up Loretta's window while Loretta stared back at Carrie, reading the words on her lips: "Mom! Wait!"

17

AWESOME

Madison Square Garden was filling up fast. Predictions of twenty-two thousand rock fans filling the famous arena to capacity were proving to be true. Most of the fans were in their late teens and early twenties; they were forty-five percent male and fifty-five percent female. All were addicted to the *"Counterfeit Five"*, a band that had perfected the art of mimicking the music and antics of most modern rock groups.

The event was scheduled to begin at 8 p.m. But at 7 p.m., every seat had already been taken. The younger the fans, the more segregated their seating. Many sections of 16-and 17-year-olds were of the same gender. Rows of boys and rows of girls punctuated the tightly packed arena. In several areas, upward of three hundred girls occupied whole sections. Meanwhile, outside the famous New York City landmark, police were directing traffic as the first of the early spring stars began to shine in the dark sky above the Big Apple.

Suddenly, directly above the massive structure, a shower of light rays began to appear in the heavens. Although slight at first, it grew into a tremendous waterfall of illumination as it approached the earth.

Faster and faster, like shooting stars, the deluge plummeted toward Madison Square Garden until, with a stunning and silent explosion of light, it pierced the roof and filled the arena. Unseen by human eyes, more than two thousand heavenly souls instantly dispatched to an equal number of earth-bound youngsters.

One by one, they appeared to their mothers and fathers, extending mercy and forgiveness. Most were 3 to 6 years of age. Some were as young as 2. Waves of emotion swept through the arena as hundreds and hundreds of parents met their children for the first time.

Soon, confusion surfaced in the arena, for only the parents could see their children. As a result, they appeared to be talking to themselves. Then, as the invasion began to take hold, a second wave of aborted children arrived. Most of the young fathers were stunned and speechless. The mothers seemed to be having an easier time of adjusting.

A 20-year-old Puerto Rican mother picked up her 2-year-old and hugged her without speaking. The tears streaming down her face said it all. A 3-year-old boy sat in his mother's lap as she rocked him back and forth, sobbing and singing praises to God for His mercy. "Oh, thank You, dear God, thank You," she cried as she looked heavenward. "I have been praying for you, little child, for three years. I have named you. I have been afraid that you were angry with me."

"Don't worry, Mommy, I love you," he said as he hugged her back. "I love you, Mommy."

Another mother, 17 at most, objected as her 2-year-old son tried to convince her he was real.

"I don't believe you. You must belong to someone else, little boy. I never had an abortion. So you don't have to forgive me." The more she spoke, the more he began to disappear until he was finally gone.

A young man and his girlfriend sat dumbfounded as twin 4-year-old girls appeared and hugged them. Surprised, he questioned them: "Where did you come from, little girls? You have to be 16 to be admitted to the concert."

"We came from Heaven, Daddy," one replied.

Laughing, he turned to his girlfriend, who was stone–faced, with a knowing look in her already tearing eyes.

"What?" he blurted in surprise.

"David," she responded as she tried to stop the flood of tears. "Don't you remember? Four years ago? Twins? The clinic?"

Wide-eyed and stunned, the young man covered his 19-year-old face with his hands

"Oh, No! No! No! No! It can't be! Please! It can't be!"

"Yes, Daddy. It is us, and we have come to help you heal. We have brought God's mercy and forgiveness to you and Mommy."

The trembling young mother reached for her children, who climbed into her lap. Rejoicing at her first opportunity to hug her daughters, she cried, "Oh, thank You, dear Lord Jesus. You have answered my prayers. I can see and touch my little ones."

Then, as she squeezed her children and pressed her cheek to theirs, she sobbed, "Children . . . I am so sorry I rejected you."

Overwhelmed, the young father cried, "What about me?" as he reached for his little girls. Instantly, they jumped into his arms as their mother willingly shared them.

"Why did we ever do that? Why?" he lamented as he also sobbed in grateful joy.

The confusion within the arena grew more profound as several thousand tearful and rejoicing youngsters went on talking to the children only they could see.

Many were addressing those sitting next to them.

"Abortion is murder!"

"It's really a baby!"

"Don't let it happen to you!"

"I can't believe we did that!"

"Tell your parents. They'll understand. They'll help you!"

Suddenly, the beautiful rejoicing was interrupted as the *"Counterfeit Five"* blasted onto the stage with their latest hit, *"Buzz Off! It's My Life!"*

18

SECOND CHANCE

Nancy dialed the intercom to Marty's office.

"O'Shea."

"Marty! How is Sarah?"

"Well, Nancy . . . she's a little better. I think it's time more than anything."

"Has she mentioned Melissa?"

"Not a word. She has, however, been looking at pictures of the kids when they were toddlers. They're in college now, but for some reason she keeps looking at their kindergarten pictures."

"She must be making a connection with Melissa," Nancy suggested.

Marty was silent.

"Are you there, Marty?"

"Yes. Yes, I'm here, Nancy. I was just thinking of my poor child Melissa and where she might be now. And if I'll ever see her again."

"Well, Marty, if all that you say about Jesus and forgiveness and salvation is true, then you will most certainly see her again."

"I want to see her now! I don't want to have to wait till I die. And I want Sarah to see her, too. If only she hadn't rejected her so forcefully."

"She was in shock, Marty. After all, she was the mother who aborted her child. It is different for the mother than it is for the father. She had to request the abortion and allow the doctor to kill her child."

"Don't minimize my pain, Nancy. I suggested the abortion. Sarah never would have thought of it on her own. I'm just as guilty as Sarah. I . . ." Marty's voice trailed off as he began to weep quietly.

"Marty, look, I will pray that Melissa comes back. I'm not religious, but I chose not to kill my child two days ago, and maybe God is happy with me."

"Please Nancy, that would be very nice of you. Please pray."

"Dear God . . . I don't know You very well. I

have not been a person of prayer during my life. But if a polite request is ok, then I will make it now. Marty is heartbroken. You gave him the beautiful gift of seeing his daughter Melissa. He loves her and is very remorseful of having aborted her. He needs her back. Sarah has rejected her and doesn't seem to be remorseful, but I think in time she will be. Sarah needs another chance. I don't ask for anything for myself, I only ask for Marty and Sarah. I don't think I'm supposed to bargain with You, but I will say that I did not abort the baby in my womb. It is the result of rape, and I never intended to have this child. But I will carry it to term. Also, and this is where the bargaining part comes in, I will forgive the rapist if You send Melissa back. And I..."

Nancy paused. She sensed that she was offending God.

"No. Change that . . . I will forgive the rapist . . . anyway. You don't have to send Melissa back, but I pray that You do. And because this prayer is for Marty and Sarah, I will add that I pray this prayer in the name of Jesus."

"Amen!" Marty answered with great enthusiasm. "Gee, that was great, Nancy. I really appreciate that. I'm going home at 4:00 today and will try to convince Sarah to pray for Melissa's return. That might be a good time for you to pray again, if you remember."

"Sure thing Marty, I'll remember."

---------- ------ ------------

Three hours later, Marty locked his office and headed for the parking garage. As he exited the elevator, he sensed a familiar light beginning to glow beside him. As he continued toward his car, the light became brighter and more distinct.

Remembering Melissa's first appearance, Marty stopped and excitedly asked, "Melissa, is it you?"

"Yes, Daddy."

Marty was ecstatic. "Oh, thank you, Melissa for coming back," he said. "I have been praying for your return. Where are you? I can't see you."

"I am in the light, Daddy, but I don't want you to see me."

"Why? You know I love you."

"Because I have been crying and I look awful. It would be too upsetting for you."

"That's ok, honey. I can handle it. I just want to be with you."

"Are you sure, Daddy?"

"Yes, I'm sure, Melissa."

"Ok, Daddy. If you're sure."

Marty smiled as Melissa's light grew brighter and began to take the shape of a 5-year-old girl. Gradually he was able to make out her features and familiar blond hair. Then suddenly he gasped in shock. Melissa's eyes were almost completely swollen shut from two days of crying.

"I told you Daddy. I look terrible"

Marty composed himself and reached to pick Melissa up but she backed away.

"Daddy you don't have to look at me."

"Melissa, honey, I love you. You are beautiful to me."

Melissa hesitated, then suddenly she threw herself into Marty's arms.

"Can we go see Mommy, Daddy? I want to hug her, too."

"Yes, sweetheart", Marty replied as he wiped a tear from his eye. "We are going to see her right now."

As Marty turned onto the freeway, Melissa began to quiz him about Sarah.

"Daddy, do you know why Mommy doesn't love me?"

"Mommy does love you, honey. She was just so surprised to see you that she couldn't handle it."

"Well, do you think she will want to see me now?"

"I'm sure she will if we give her a few minutes to adjust.

"Father is letting Mommy see me so she will repent and be at peace with Him. He is very merciful and forgiving. He wants to hug Mommy too. She is His child."

Marty rounded the last turn as he headed down his street.

"There's the house, Daddy."

Melissa closed her eyes and began to pray.

"Dear Father, please touch Mommy's heart. Please don't let her reject me again. Please save her from unhappiness. Help her to accept the truth. Thank You. Amen."

Marty wiped a tear from his eye and turned into the driveway.

Before he could open his door, Melissa jumped out of the car and ran to the front porch.

"No! Melissa, honey . . . wait. Please wait. Let me prepare Mommy."

Melissa stopped and turned back toward Marty.

"How can you prepare her, Daddy?"

"I'll just go inside and tell her that you have come back and want to see her."

"Ok, Daddy, but please hurry."

Marty turned the front door handle and quietly walked into the house. He found Sarah standing at the kitchen counter reading a recipe.

"Hi, honey. How was work?"

Marty didn't answer. Sarah looked up.

"What's the matter, Marty?"

"Sarah, honey . . . we've been given another chance."

"What do you mean 'another chance'?"

Marty didn't respond, but looked pensively at the floor.

Sarah looked suspiciously toward the front door.

"Marty,... you don't mean that. . . ?"

Marty looked directly at Sarah.

"Yes. She has returned."

Sarah put the cookbook down and pulled out a chair from the table.

"I can't do this, Marty. I can't do this . . . this is insanity. She must be some lost child. She can't possibly be from Heaven. She isn't our daughter."

Marty remained silent.

"What does she look like? Maybe she is one of those missing children that are on display at the post office."

Sarah stood up and walked toward the front door. "Is she outside?"

Marty nodded.

"Was she waiting here when you drove in?"

"No. She came with me from the office."

"Marty, if she is someone's lost child, they could accuse you of kidnaping."

Marty didn't respond.

Sarah glanced at the coffee table, where the album she had been perusing for the last two days was lying open. Next to the pictures of her two children was a snapshot of herself at age 5. She was being pushed on a swing by her father, and only her back and her long blond hair were visible. She pulled the picture from the album which revealed another picture of herself she had hidden there years before. Marty had taken the picture of her in her maternity outfit a few days before the abortion. Shocked to see it again she picked it up and clutched both pictures as she slowly walked to the front door. Cautiously turning the handle she inched the door open as her eyes wandered down the driveway to Marty's car.

There, standing with her back to the house, was Melissa. Sarah noticed her long blond hair. It was surprisingly similar to her own at the same age. Anxious and very tense, Sarah stepped onto the front porch and walked slowly down the steps. Fifty feet down the driveway was a child who could be her own.

Suddenly Sarah heard a whisper from Marty twenty feet behind her.

"Be patient...she thinks you don't love her."

Sarah turned and faced Marty. She tried to speak but lost her voice. Tears poured from her eyes as she reached for him. Marty rushed to her and embraced her just as Melissa turned and faced them. She, too, was weeping.

"Mommy, I love you. I just want to hug you. You don't have to hug me back if you don't want to."

Still unsure, Sarah looked at the picture of herself when almost five months pregnant. Struggling to speak she turned from Marty's embrace and forced herself to look at Melissa. Instantly she lost her balance and stumbled. Marty caught her and eased her to the ground.

"Oh, dear God, you poor child," Sarah moaned as she bravely tried to look at Melissa whose eyes were almost completely closed from crying. "Forgive me . . . forgive me . . . I am so sorry," she sobbed as she placed her head in her hands and wept.

"I forgive you, Mommy. I do . . . I do forgive you. I love you."

Sarah reached up to embrace Melissa, and Melissa fell into her arms. Rocking back and forth, Sarah held Melissa close to her heart, repeating, "I love you, I love you," as Melissa and Marty wept with her.

When Sarah tried to clear her eyes and look at Melissa again, she suddenly shouted for joy.

"Oh, you are so beautiful. You are such a beautiful child. Melissa, I love you!

Melissa raised her eyes and hands to heaven. "Thank You, dear God, our Father," she prayed. "Thank You for helping Mommy. She is happy now. Thank You, Father. We love You."

Marty put his arms around Melissa and Sarah, rejoicing in the victory of love. Together, they held onto one another for an earthly eternity.

19

WOUNDED VICTIMS

Vicki maneuvered her sedan into the right-hand lane of FDR Drive. She had to take the next exit, as she and Loretta were approaching the U.N. from the north.

For the last five miles, Vicki had been unsuccessful at getting any information from Loretta about the tall young lady she had been speaking with on the street corner. Each time she mentioned it, Loretta would change the subject.

Several blocks later, Vicki worked her way through the complex security system in the lower level of the U.N. parking garage. Suddenly, Loretta asked that Vicki let her out by the elevator, saying she wanted to get to her desk early.

"Sure, Loretta," Vicki replied as the car came to a stop. "I'll meet you upstairs as soon as I park."

Loretta jumped out and walked to the elevator lobby. Still thinking about the encounter on the corner, she asked herself, "How could that young lady know that I had an abortion? That was thirty-two years ago. She probably wasn't even born at the time."

Once upstairs, Loretta began to arrange her personal belongings into several small moving boxes that she had purchased for her special "retirement move." Tomorrow was the day.

"Hey, Loretta. I'll bet you're looking forward to your last day of work," Danny Conners shouted as he passed Loretta's desk pushing the break wagon.

"Oh, hi, Danny. Yes, I sure am. Oh, please let me have two coffees and two bagels. Onion for me and plain for Vicki."

"Sure thing, Loretta."

As Loretta tried to give Danny a $10 bill, he pushed his cart down the hallway.

"It's on the house, Loretta. That's my going-away present. I'll see you tomorrow before you leave."

"Oh, Danny, thank you. That is very thoughtful," Loretta called.

"He's always been a nice guy," Loretta reflected as she looked across the office at the desks of her friends for more than forty years. Most of them had pictures of family members on their desks, which always gave her a sense of well-being. Her own desk held a picture of her brother and his wife and children.

As Loretta looked at the picture, she noticed that her oldest niece, now 27 years of age but 16 in the picture, bore a striking similarity to the young lady she had met that morning. The more she looked, the more she wanted to look.

"That girl said her name was Carrie. She looks very similar to my niece, Susan. She said she was my daughter. That she was from Heaven. . ."

Loretta sat down. She felt confused and a bit upset at the possibility that Carrie might be her daughter and could have come from Heaven.

"Ridiculous," she audibly said to herself. "Absolutely ridiculous."

"What's ridiculous?" Vicki asked as she rounded the hallway turn and approached her desk.

"Oh, hi, Vicki. I . . . uh . . . I was just thinking out load. But, I'm also thinking that it is ridiculous that I have spent so many years here and everything I have accumulated will fit into three small boxes."

"Yeah, I know. I'll be right behind you in two more years. Thirty is enough for me. I don't know how you made it through forty-three years. Oh, Loretta, we never got to finish that conversation as we drove in this morning. Who did you say that young lady was? She looked very similar to you."

"Similar to me! Are you serious?"

"Yes. She was about the same height. Very similar features and she definitely had your smile, although you didn't seem to be smiling yourself. Was she a relative?"

Loretta was becoming anxious. The thought of Carrie really being her daughter was a frightening possibility, and she didn't want to deal with it. Not now!

"No! Uh...not really Vicki. I have only one niece and she lives in Texas."

"Well, if she's not your niece, who is she?"

Loretta became silent and sat down. Staring at the picture of her brother's family, she made a feeble effort to respond. In little more than a whisper she replied, "I'm not sure."

Vicki sat down at her desk and looked

directly at Loretta. "Are you ok? You've been acting a little bit unusual today."

"FIFTEEN MINUTES UNTIL ASSEMBLY," the loudspeaker blasted across the translators' office complex. Hurriedly, more than two hundred U.N. translators began to make their way to the elevators to begin another day of bringing the nations of the world together in their native tongues. Loretta and Vicki made their way with the crowd to the elevators.

"We can talk about this on the way home, Vicki. I'll be having lunch today with the Chilean ambassador. He wants to thank me for my help in teaching him English."

"Sure, Loretta. I understand. I'll see you tonight."

As Loretta made her way to her translator's station, she was hoping for a delay in the proceedings. It would give her a chance to make a fast phone call to the doorman at her apartment building to see whether Carrie was still around. As she sat down, she could see that her monitor was not illuminated, which meant she had at least fifteen minutes before translating, so she quickly dialed her building. Her hand seemed to tremble as she pushed the doorman's extension number on the keypad.

"James! May I help you?"

"James . . . this is Loretta Brown."

"Yes, Mrs. Brown."

"Have you seen Carrie since early this morning?"

"Oh, you mean your daughter? Uh, no, I haven't seen her since she was speaking with you on the corner. If I do see her, is there any message?"

"Well . . . no. No message. Thank you, James."

Loretta hung up. Silent and pensive, she tapped her fingers on the desk as she replayed the scene on the street corner an hour earlier.

"Could she really be my daughter? Could she have survived the abortion? I was almost six months pregnant. Even if she survived, how could she have known who she was? And why would the clinic not have informed me? Her story about coming from Heaven is ridiculous. She must be a con artist who looks up medical records and tries to swindle people."

Yellow lights began to blink on hundreds of monitors as the opening of the Wednesday session approached. Loretta arranged her headset and readied herself for another day of translating.

———— ——— ————

      Lunchtime at the United Nations was a bit different from that of many companies in New York where most people hit the streets and went to their favorite restaurants. The U.N. boasted a very elaborate cafeteria and the majority of the employees patronized the facility.

      Today, however, would be different for Loretta. The Chilean ambassador was treating her to a private lunch at the Ambassadors' Club near the U.N. His wife, Elizabeth, and daughter, Julie, would be joining them. All three had become very proficient in English thanks to the extensive time Loretta had spent teaching them.

      As the morning session came to a close, Loretta put down her headset and returned to her office complex to prepare for lunch. Minutes later, she said goodbye to Vicki and departed for the main lobby, where she would meet Ambassador Eduardo Cortez.

      As she stepped off the elevator, Eduardo spotted her and came to greet her with a warm embrace, followed by his wife and daughter.

      "Thank you for joining us, Loretta," Elizabeth said as she, too, embraced her.

      "Oh, it is so nice to see you all, and thank

you for inviting me," Loretta replied as they made their way to the street.

"It's only two blocks to the club, Loretta," the ambassador offered as he pointed the way. "Just a short walk."

As they approached the street corner, Loretta gasped. Carrie was walking toward her on the sidewalk in front of the Ambassadors' Club. With Carrie staring directly at her, Loretta panicked and slowed down, allowing the others to pass her.

"Hi, Mom!" Carrie called. "I was just on my way to surprise you for lunch."

Speechless, Loretta fumbled for a response, but the ambassador spoke first.

"Oh, what a surprise, Loretta, I didn't know you had a daughter. How do you do, young lady, my name is Eduardo Cortez, and this is my wife, Elizabeth, and daughter, Julie."

"How do you do, Mr. Cortez, Elizabeth, and Julie. I'm Carrie Brown. It is very nice meeting you."

"Loretta, why did you keep secret such a beautiful daughter? It's amazing how she looks so much like you," Elizabeth exclaimed.

Loretta struggled for a breath to respond. Suddenly, she found herself blurting, "Oh, I guess

I'm just becoming absent–minded."

"Well, Carrie, we would love to have you join us for lunch if you have the time," Elizabeth invited.

"Oh, I don't want to impose—"

"No imposition whatsoever, Carrie," the ambassador interrupted as he put his arm around Carrie's shoulder and ushered the ladies inside the club.

As the head waiter led them to their table, Loretta felt her hands trembling as Carrie walked in front of her.

"This can't be happening," Loretta said to herself as they were being seated. "This isn't real. She could not be my daughter. My daughter died in the abortion."

Suddenly, in an effort to avert any conversation about Carrie, she changed the subject. "Gee, I feel like royalty," Loretta remarked to Elizabeth.

Smiling, Elizabeth replied, "Actually royalty frequently comes here for lunch and dinner. We might even see someone today."

"Well, Carrie is a 'royal' surprise," the ambassador insisted as he smiled at Loretta.

"Well, yes, yes . . . thank you, Mr. Ambassador," Loretta nervously replied.

"Please, Loretta, after all these years, feel free to call me Ed. Titles are just a professional courtesy, but we are friends."

"Well, thank you, Ed. I will try to remember."

"What will you have for lunch today, Julie, dear?" the ambassador asked his teenage daughter as he looked around the table.

"Gee, Dad . . . I'm not really feeling that great. . . . I think I'll have a light salad and maybe some iced tea."

"Oh, I'm sorry to hear that. Nothing serious, I trust."

"Uh . . . she's ok, Ed, honey," Elizabeth interrupted. "She'll be fine. She's just a bit under the weather and—"

"Excuse me, Mom, but I'm old enough to speak for myself," Julie complained. "It's not quite as simple as being 'a bit under the weather,' Dad, but I'm sure in time I'll be back to my normal self."

Somewhat surprised at Julie's vague response, Eduardo sat back in his chair.

"Julie dear," he asked quietly, "is there anything I need to know to help you?"

Julie looked quietly at the tablecloth as the waiter poured her water. Gently she wiped a tear from her eye.

"No. That's ok, Dad. . . . I'll be fine in time."

"May I take your order?" the waiter asked.

"Uh . . . yes, please," Elizabeth responded in a louder-than-usual voice in an apparent effort to change the somber mood.

While Elizabeth ordered, Eduardo leaned toward his daughter and whispered as he put his arm around her shoulder.

Then, after everyone had ordered, the ambassador addressed Loretta.

"Loretta, you have labored for many years at the United Nations. What are your plans for retirement?"

"Well, Ed, I think I will just relax for the first few weeks before I investigate various charitable organizations to see if I can volunteer my time in some productive way."

"Wonderful, Loretta. That is very much in keeping with your personality. Any idea what type of charity?"

"Well, not really, Ed. I think I will just keep an open mind."

"How about one of the Right to Life organizations, Mom?" Carrie suggested. "They are usually very active."

Stunned, Loretta groped for words.

"Uh, yes . . . I suppose that is a consideration."

"They work very hard to educate society about euthanasia, the death penalty, and abortion," Carrie continued.

Suddenly, Elizabeth put her arm around Julie as she began to weep quietly.

"Oh, Julie, sweetheart, what is the trouble?" Eduardo exclaimed as he shuffled his chair next to her.

"It's nothing, Ed," Elizabeth objected. "She'll be fine."

"No, I Won't be fine, Mom . . . I won't be fine," Julie cried as she burst into tears and buried her face in her napkin.

Embarrassed at the outburst, the ambassador began to converse with Loretta and Carrie as Elizabeth comforted Julie.

"So, Carrie, you were saying that pro-life volunteers are very active."

"Yes, ambassador. They are very dedicated to helping women realize that abortion is not just the removal of tissue as so many clinics claim, but that it is the actual killing of a child."

"Well, what about early on, at just a few months?" the curious ambassador continued.

"The baby's heart is beating just three weeks after conception," Carrie forcefully responded.

"Three weeks?" a stunned Eduardo exclaimed. "Are you sure?"

"Absolutely. It is an acknowledged fact. Medical science established that years ago."

"Well, then, how could anyone go forward with such a thing?" he complained.

"Stop! Stop! I don't want to hear any more," Julie cried as she openly wept. "I can't handle another word of it. I had...an abortion...yesterday! Please stop talking about it!"

Suddenly, Loretta pushed her chair back and walked over to Julie, putting her hand on her shoulder.

"Julie, a woman has a right to an abortion. It is her choice. It is legal and necessary at times."

Ambassador Cortez was bewildered and embarrassed as he noticed many of the patrons watching this unfolding spectacle. He motioned to the waiter and said, "Please excuse us. We will be leaving."

The waiter nodded and held the ladies' chairs. As they reached the sidewalk, the ambassador whispered to Loretta, "I am so sorry,

Loretta. Please stay in touch. We will have another time together in the near future."

Once the ambassador and his family were at a distance, Loretta turned to Carrie. "How could you have been so tactless," she admonished. "It was obvious that poor child was upset about something."

"Well, I didn't know she had an abortion, Mom. But even so, we must speak the truth no matter what."

"Well, let me tell you something about truth, young lady . . . whoever you are. The truth is that abortion is a woman's right. It is her body and it is nobody's business."

"No, it isn't her body, Mom. It is the baby's body. And I'm your baby."

"No, you are not. You are not my baby. Now go away and leave me alone."

Stunned, Carrie stepped back as Loretta pushed her way past and stormed back to the U.N. It was almost time for the afternoon session.

20

MOMENT OF TRUTH

The Senate chamber was silent as the opening session roll call continued. For senior members, it was a familiar procedure, but for the freshman senators, it was a new and exciting experience. For the first time ever, they would hear their names announced in the United States Senate and would respond as senators.

This session, sixteen new members had taken their places among the veterans, and fully fourteen of them had been elected on pro-life platforms. For the pro-life movement, this was a national victory. Years of praying and sacrifice had yielded results far beyond anyone's expectations. Many races had resulted in upsets. The incoming pro-lifers included nine women and five men.

Today, the much-anticipated vote on the "Life at Conception Act" was to be taken. Because of the bill's historical significance, the gallery was filled to capacity. The major networks were carrying the proceedings live throughout the day. If the bill passed it would declare that "human life begins at conception, from the moment of fertilization," and is therefore protected by the 14th Amendment to The United States Constitution.

Seated at the back of the chamber was a group of disabled young Americans known as "Disabled Youth for Life." Many had suffered serious injuries that had left them paralyzed, while others had been disabled since birth. They came from virtually every state in the Union and represented many churches, synagogues, and houses of worship. Their alliance was formed by their collective concern for life in the womb. In America, abortion was the greatest threat to that life.

"My fellow senators," the presiding senator called out. "The roll call is complete. Let us please stand and welcome our sixteen newly elected colleagues'."

Every member of the United States Senate

stood and applauded as the new senators humbly acknowledged their acceptance. Gradually, one by one, all took their seats and listened attentively as the agenda was read before the chamber.

"Looks like it's going to be a busy day," Ellie Green said to her fifty-seven fellow Disabled Youth for Life members, most of who were in wheelchairs. "According to the agenda, they won't take up the 'Life at Conception Act" until after lunch. And from what I've been told, 'after lunch' could mean early evening."

"I've heard the same thing," Pedro Tarafa replied. Pedro had lost both of his lower legs in the Iraq war and was still in physical therapy. He was hoping to regain control of his life through the use of artificial limbs. "That should give us plenty of time for prayer."

Pedro had taught the group his favorite prayer, The Chaplet of the Divine Mercy, which he had learned in Baghdad. The chaplet was recited for the benefit of the sick and dying. Although it was a Christian prayer, every member, regardless of religious preference, was very comfortable with it.

As the day wore on, the Senate became embroiled in debates regarding several bills.

According to the agenda, the senators were considerably behind schedule, and there was even talk of tabling the "Life at Conception Act" until the next day.

As they broke for lunch, the chamber quickly became deserted except for a few small groups of senators gathered together. Because of the lack of people in the chamber, the senators' voices easily carried to the rear, where the disabled youth were gathered.

"We can't table it until tomorrow, Harry," one senator said. "We might lose two or three votes in the process, and then it will be too close to call. Besides, we aren't positive how some of the freshmen will behave if the voting is close. We know what they say, but what they do may be another matter."

"You're right, John," another senator replied. "That's what happened four years ago. We'd better push for a vote today and hope for the best."

As the senators filed out of the chamber, most went to the cafeteria, where heated discussions were already taking place regarding the "Life at Conception Act." Advocates for abortion rights were demanding that a woman has a right to do with her own body as she chooses.

"No one has a right to tell a woman what she can and cannot do with her own body" a northern Senator asserted.

"The purpose of this bill, Senator, is to protect young Americans as they grow in their mothers' wombs," the junior senator from Florida insisted. "This bill has nothing to do with the mother's body. But it has everything to do with the child's body, and that child could be a female. And as you suggest Senator, 'a woman has a right to do with her own body as she chooses'. And these female children choose to live."

The northern Senator abruptly pushed his chair from the table and moved to another on the opposite side of the dining room. Most of those sitting at the new table shared his ideology regarding abortion, except for two who identified themselves as pro-life, but who occasionally voted against pro-life measures.

As the northern Senator engaged his colleagues, a captivating glow began to surround the table. Gradually, the conversation was replaced by silent curiosity as the illumination grew in size and intensity. Suddenly, small children appeared within the light, causing silent panic among all those at the table. Elsewhere in the dining room, similar encounters with children were taking place. However, none of the pro-life senators could see or understand what was happening. Only the pro-abortion senators were experiencing the apparitions. Some were even being addressed by the children.

"But, senator, I had a right to life just as my mother did," one child said to a senator.

"Why tell me?" he replied. "I didn't abort you."

"Because, you are about to vote to stop a bill that will save my brothers and sisters from death by abortion."

"I am free to vote as I choose and a woman is free to do as she chooses with her own body. That's the law."

"It is not Father's law, senator, and—"

"Who are you talking to, senator?" the waiter asked as he offered the menu.

Throughout the dining room, many similar encounters were taking place, confusing the waiters and pro-life senators. Several pro-abortion female senators were weeping, as were a half-dozen men.

As the confusion continued and threatened to derail the remainder of the business day, the apparitions suddenly ceased. Conversation eventually took hold again and the lunch hour resumed.

By 2 p.m., the afternoon session was in full swing and several pro-life senators were lining up to speak regarding the "Life at Conception Act." A freshman senator from South Carolina had a surprise scheduled for the end of his comments to the chamber. At present, he was huddled with the "Disabled Youth for Life" members at the rear of the chamber.

At 4 p.m., the announcement came that the vote for the "Life at Conception Act" would be held following commentary. One by one, the opposing sides sent their representatives to the podium, and one by one they were applauded and booed by friend and foe.

A pro-abortion western senator took the podium and railed against the pro-life senators for interfering with a woman's right to choose. She was followed immediately by the freshman senator from South Carolina. After thanking his fellow senators for their warm welcome earlier in the day, he adopted a more serious tone.

"My distinguished colleagues. We have heard much commentary from both perspectives regarding the "Life at Conception Act." One phrase that is repeatedly uttered by those against this bill is "A woman's right to choose." I ask you ... **CHOOSE WHAT?"**

The chamber was unusually quiet as the young senator stared steely-eyed at the western senator.

"If you mean 'choose abortion' then you should have the courage to say so. And if you say abortion, then you should give us a full understanding of what abortion is. For those involved in abortion, there is a common understanding that abortion is a violent act that kills a baby. And yet, you say a woman has a right to choose. Well, for your information, abortion doesn't *always* kill a baby. Sometimes that baby survives abortion. Such was the experience of a young Hispanic child eleven years ago in Texas.

"Most of you have heard about little Angelina Hernandez. But most of you have never met her."

As the freshman senator continued speaking, a young girl in the back of the chamber began to move toward the podium in her wheelchair. Slowly, she became visible to the full governmental body as she wheeled closer and closer to the podium. Silence permeated the senate chamber as never before. No one moved or uttered a word as the pretty little crippled girl struggled to pull herself up on her crutches and walk to the podium. She was barely able to ascend the steps, so two Senate pages rushed to her side and assisted her to the podium.

"For those of you who have not met Angelina, I introduce her to you now," the South Carolina senator said.

Shocked, and uncertain how to respond, the entire assembly remained absolutely silent as Angelina shuffled closer to the microphone. With her right hand, she pulled the microphone closer to her face while supporting herself with what remained of her left arm.

"My name is Angelina Hernandez," she began. "I survived my abortion eleven years ago. After cutting off my left arm and both my feet, the doctor pulled me from my mother's womb and threw me into a plastic bag. Minutes later, a nurse passing the medical waste department noticed my movements in the bag and saved my life. As you can see, my face was disfigured and I am blind in my left eye. But I am alive. And—"

Angelina began to lose her voice as tears came to her eyes.

"And I ask you . . . please let my brothers and sisters live. Don't kill any more of us in abortion. We are Americans too, and want to live just like you."

Angelina tried to wipe the tears from her eyes with her right hand, but she kept losing her balance as they rolled down her face. She struggled to continue.

"Your life... and my life, are gifts from God. Do we want to break His heart again and again by killing His children? He is so patient. So loving. So kind. Won't you please consider Him. Please... Please vote for life. Vote yes for the "Life at Conception Act."

Most of the chamber was in tears. The western senator put her head in her hands and wept. Then, as Angelina turned to leave the podium, her prosthetic feet came into view, further crushing the Senate members. As she hobbled across the stage on her crutches, one hundred United States senators stood cheering and applauding amid their tears. By the time she had wheeled herself to the rear of the assembly, a somber senator had walked to the podium.

"Ladies and gentlemen, no further commentary will be necessary. We have heard enough from all concerned. It is time to vote."

As the full United States Senate began to cast their votes, fifty-seven members of Disabled

Youth for Life gathered around Pedro as he led them in reciting The Chaplet of Divine Mercy.

"Eternal Father, we offer you the body and blood, soul and Divinity of Your Dearly Beloved Son Our Lord Jesus Christ in atonement for our sins and those of the whole world.
For the sake of His Sorrowful Passion have mercy on us and on the whole world."

Their prayer continued throughout the voting process.

21

SAVING GRACE

The setting sun gently glistened on the brass arms of the ornate Central Park bench. Carrie waited patiently, hoping to see Vicki's car approaching Loretta's apartment building. Her plan was to rush across the street and meet her mother as the doorman opened the car door. Carrie was beginning to experience human depression, something she had warned her fellow pilgrims about but had not fully understood. Now, as the pain began to settle deep within her heart, the experience explained more than words were able.

"Suppose she doesn't accept me again?" Carrie thought. "Suppose she outright rejects me even though she believes I'm from Heaven?

Tears began to form in Carrie's eyes as she sadly bowed her head and began to pray silently.

"Dear Father. It was easy for me to encourage the others. But now it's my turn and I'm not doing very well. Please help me to convince Mom to accept my forgiveness. Please help her to believe in Your mercy and love. I know You are always with me, but right now I'm feeling very alone."

Immediately, a soft and reassuring light surrounded Carrie. Instinctively she raised her hands toward Heaven as the light grew brighter.

"Praise You, Father. I trust You."

Suddenly Carrie's guardian emerged from the light in a magnificent glow of beauty. As he gently touched the top of her head, she, too, began to beam brightly. A trusting smile enveloped her face as she quietly wept in the great joy of Heaven.

"Oh, thank You. Thank You, Father, for reassuring me. I love You and trust You. I will persevere. I will not retreat. I will continue to pray. Please help Mom to believe in Your mercy and forgiveness."

At that very moment, high above the earth, a multitude of pilgrims was praying fervently for Loretta as she and Vicki made their way north during rush hour. Usually a very vocal person, Loretta was great company for Vicki, who liked interesting conversation. Today, however, was different. Today Loretta hadn't spoken since they pulled out of the U.N. garage. She and Vicki had been riding together for many years, and quiet moments like these were very rare. Looking at her pensive friend, Vicki said, "Loretta, you must be deep in thought about tomorrow, your last day at work."

"Well, somewhat I guess, Vicki. I just have a lot on my mind."

"What else could be occupying your thoughts? I have never seen you so silent. Could it be that young lady you were speaking with when I picked you up this morning?"

"Oh . . . uh . . . well, maybe. Anything is possible, I suppose."

"Come on, Loretta. I have known you for thirty years. Something is bugging you. How about trusting an old friend and sharing it with me."

"It's nothing, Vicki, I. . . ." Loretta started to speak but suddenly lost her voice. Unable to continue, she put her hand to her mouth.

Stunned, Vicki turned away and stared at the stalled traffic in front of her. Whispering, she replied, "Loretta, honey . . . I'm here for you. No matter what it is, I'm ready to listen."

Loretta began to weep quietly. She struggled to speak, but repeatedly failed. Vicki patiently waited. Several miles of silence ensued as the traffic crept along FDR Drive. Gradually, Loretta was able to compose herself.

"Vicki . . . I have never shared this with anyone. Not another soul on the face of the earth. And I never intended to speak about it . . . ever."

"It's ok, Loretta, you don't have to tell—"

"No. No . . . Vicki, I do want to. I need to."

Loretta wiped the tears from her eyes and regained her courage.

"Before I met you, Vicki, I had a relationship with a man. We lived together at my apartment and everyone there thought we were married. I believed he loved me, and although we talked about marriage, it never came to pass. He was very personable and very generous. He worked in the intelligence department on the tenth floor and had been there for several years before we met. Well . . . then . . . uh. . . ." Loretta became emotional again and put a tissue to her eyes.

"It's ok, Loretta . . . take your time. You're

doing fine," Vicki assured.

"Well . . . wouldn't you know . . . I became pregnant . . . and for some reason I never told him until I was five months along. I was so naturally thin that it was barely noticeable. When I finally decided it was time to tell him, I sat him down at the kitchen table and looked him directly in the eye. As soon as I finished he reacted with shock. He said he didn't want any part of being a father, and several days later he announced he was moving out. Eventually he left the U.N. and I never saw him again. When he moved out, I panicked and decided to get an abortion. I was almost six months pregnant at the time. I have tried to forget the abortion for thirty-two years. Sometimes the memories give me trouble. Then today's strange encounter with that young woman who insisted she was my daughter and had come back from Heaven to forgive me."

"What! She said what?" Vicki interrupted.

"She said she was my daughter. Her name is Carrie Brown. She said she had come from Heaven to forgive me. She said God loves me and forgives me and wants me to repent and accept His mercy."

"That is ridiculous. Don't pay any attention to her. You'll probably never see her again."

"I didn't think I would see her again, either. But today at lunch with the ambassador, she showed up outside the club and joined us. There was a scene with his daughter and the lunch was cancelled. Later, outside on the sidewalk, she insisted once again that she was my daughter. I told her she was not my daughter and walked away from her. Now . . . now I don't know what to think."

Loretta appeared haggard and very drained.

"Loretta . . . be peaceful. This whole thing is absurd. The past is the past and nobody comes back from Heaven. This young lady is a fake."

Patiently waiting outside Loretta's building Carrie wiped the tears from her face as she spotted Vicki's car approaching. While the doorman made his way to the curb, Carrie bolted across the street. She arrived just as her mother stepped out.

"Mom! I've been waiting for you—"

"No . . . Leave me alone . . . Go away," Loretta pleaded as she stepped from the car. "You're upsetting me."

"But Mom, I just want to talk to you for a few minutes."

"Young lady, leave Loretta alone," Vicki insisted as she jumped from behind the wheel and confronted Carrie on the sidewalk. "You are not her daughter."

"Yes, I am. Look at me."

Vicki was silent as she looked directly at Loretta and Carrie standing next to each other. Their resemblance was striking. Vicki was speechless, not knowing whether Loretta was telling her the truth. Could she have really given birth to Carrie but placed her in adoption because she wasn't married? Could Carrie be her niece?

"Mom . . . I forgive you. *Please* accept my forgiveness. I love you and God loves you. He forgives you. Please repent and accept His mercy."

Suddenly, Loretta stood very straight and mustered all her strength.

"James, please make this woman leave us alone."

"Yes, Mrs. Brown. You will have to leave young lady or I will summon the police."

"No, Mom, please . . . please . . . I love you," Carrie cried as a dim light began to surround her.

"What is happening to you?" Vicki shouted as she watched Carrie's appearance change.

"I am being rejected again as I was on the day of my abortion. If I am accepted and Mom seeks God's forgiveness, I will be allowed to spend some time with her. If she continues to reject me I will be called back."

"I am not your mother. Go away!"

Carrie burst into tears as the light grew brighter and she became less visible. James and Vicki began to back away from Carrie.

"What is happening here?" Vicki demanded again as a frightened James ran into the lobby to call the police.

"I told you," Carrie cried. "If Mom doesn't accept me, I will be returned."

"Stop calling me Mom and go away. I don't want you," Loretta insisted.

Overcome with grief, Carrie turned and ran down the street, crossing to the other side and disappearing around the corner. The faster she ran, the dimmer she became, causing shock to passers by.

Vicki turned to Loretta.

"I'm afraid, Loretta. This is scary. Do you think there could be any truth to this? I mean, she looks very much like you. Same height. Same features. Same voice."

"Are you serious? You don't mean you believe her, do you?"

"I don't know," Vicki responded. "It seems awfully convincing."

"Yes, it does," James added as he approached the ladies.

Shocked at James assertion, Loretta became very quiet. Then, in a barely audible voice, she began repeating, "No. . . . No. . . . This isn't happening. It can't be her. It was so long ago. So long ago . . . but she looked just as I did when I had the abortion. She is so much like me. I . . . ."

Loretta began to weep. She knelt to the sidewalk, put her face in her hands, and openly wept. Vicki knelt next to her and put her arms around her.

"Loretta, honey . . . it could be possible. She could be your daughter. Maybe it is God's will that this is happening."

"Why don't you go after her and catch her," James suggested. "What do you have to lose? If she is your daughter, then you will be together. If she isn't, then you can forget it."

Reaching for James hand, Loretta pulled herself upright.

"Vicki. . . . Come with me?"

"Sure."

Loretta bolted across the street, running between oncoming cars. With Vicki right on her heals, she ran around the corner, hoping to find Carrie within sight. Struggling to see between tears, Loretta panicked as the almost vacant street unfolded before her. Stopping suddenly as Vicki caught up with her she noticed a subway entrance on the other side of the street.

"Maybe she went into the subway," an almost hysterical Loretta cried.

"Let's give it a try," Vicki insisted as she pushed Loretta into the street. Together they raced toward the subway entrance, then, charged down the stairs, desperately trying to catch Carrie.

Suddenly Vicki spotted Carrie slowly walking away at the far end of the platform. She seemed to be fading in appearance.

"Wait," Loretta screamed. "Wait..."

Carrie's sobbing drowned out Loretta's voice as the light enfolding her began to lift her above the platform. The sound of Loretta's pounding feet echoed in the concrete cavern beneath the city streets as she raced to catch Carrie at the other end of the very long platform.

"No! . . . Please wait, Carrie. I'm sorry...I love you...Please forgive me! Wait...Wait...I'm trying to catch you," Loretta pleaded as she pushed herself to her physical limits.

Suddenly, Vicki stopped and knelt. "Please, dear God, let Loretta catch Carrie. Please don't take her back yet."

"Dear God, help me...Please...I want my daughter," Loretta screamed in her desperate moment of truth.

Suddenly, the light surrounding Carrie grew dimmer, and she miraculously turned to see her mother racing to catch her. With her profoundly tear filled face, she tried to smile and respond as the light of her guardian stopped ascending and returned her to the platform. Instantly she tried to run to her approaching mother, but Loretta was running so fast Carrie just held out her arms as Loretta raced the last few feet and threw herself into Carrie's embrace. Hysterically sobbing, she cried, "I've wanted to hold you every day for thirty-two years, and now I finally can. You are beautiful to me my baby. . . my baby... I love you. I am so sorry...forgive me! Please forgive me!"

"I do, Momma. . . . I do forgive you. Father sent me to bring you His mercy and—"

"Dear God, forgive me . . . I repent of having killed my child . . . please forgive me . . . I accept your mercy," Loretta pleaded as Vicki watched in amazement.

Suddenly, in a flash of light that illuminated the entire subway, Carrie was restored to her Heavenly appearance and a beautiful, tearful smile captured her face. Embracing her mother, she screamed heavenward, "Thank you, Father, thank you for saving my mother."

As Carrie's voice echoed against the walls, another sound began to take hold. It was music, but unlike any other heard on earth. Beautiful, captivating music, it gently pierced the heart as it grew louder.

Confused, Loretta stepped back from Carrie and asked, "What is it? What is happening?"

Carrie seemed to be talking, but not to Loretta.

"Yes. . . . Yes, I understand," she said as she looked Heavenward.

Slowly the light returned and enveloped Carrie.

"No, Please! . . . You're not leaving! I wanted to spend some time with you," a desperate Loretta pleaded. "Please, Carrie, stay with me... I thought you would be able to stay for a while!"

"Mom, the time for all to return has arrived. It is not my decision. Father has called every pilgrim back home."

The music grew louder and began to fill Loretta's heart with peace. She tried to embrace Carrie as she was beginning to ascend in the light, but only their hands could gently touch as she was lifted heavenward.

"I love you Mom," Carrie called. "I will be with you in Heaven."

"Child . . . Child . . . I love you. Thank you... thank you," Loretta cried as Carrie was slowly lifted out of sight.

In seconds, Carrie was high above the earth, racing to the staging area in the arms of her guardian. As she approached the massive gathering of souls, she could see millions more pouring in from every city in America. Many of them had returned to earth for a second time and now were rejoicing over their successes. Some, however, were still sad and dejected.

Standing before the beautiful blue and white silhouette of earth, Carrie reflected on the great mercy of her Father, who had extended such love and patience to His children. Turning,

she addressed her brothers and sisters who had
failed.

"Do not be discouraged if you were not
successful. Father's grace will continue to inspire
your parents' hearts. They still have the
remainder of their lives to repent. Pray that they
seek Father's mercy before their final hour."

Suddenly in a flash of light all the children
were restored to their beautiful Heavenly
condition.

Carrie then moved to the head of the
assembly and addressed her 40 million brothers
and sisters.

"And now it is time to depart. We must
kneel in silent prayer to Father and thank Him for
our individual experiences."

The universe was silent once again as each
heart and soul poured out its love, praise, and
thanksgiving to its Creator. Then, one by one,
they rose and stood in silent formation, waiting
for instructions from their leader. Moments later,
Carrie spoke:

"Rejoice, my brothers and sisters. We are
going to the home of our Father."

As God's children turned from earth and
began the journey back home, Carrie noticed an
immense movement of light coming toward

them. It grew in size and length, reaching almost to Heaven as it approached the earth. It dwarfed the size of the returning army of pilgrims as it drew alongside their column. Carrie could see that it was an army of pilgrims just like themselves.

"Where are you going?" she called to their leader.

"To earth . . . to every country but America," the leader called back.

"Why are you going?" Carrie continued.

"To bring Father's mercy to those who aborted us."

"How many are you?"

"More than One Billion," came the staggering response.

Stunned, Carrie replied, "Are you from the beginning of creation?"

"No," replied the leader. "We are from 1920 to the present."

Overwhelmed, Carrie asked, "May we pray together?"

"Please," he anxiously responded.

"Dear God, our Father, please forgive your human people. Save them from the horror of abortion and destroy the evil that tempts them toward this desperate act. Return love and obedience to their hearts so they may enjoy the life you have given them and return home with a pure soul. Please give great courage to our brothers and sisters as they make this journey. We ask this of you and thank you in the name of your Son, our Lord and Savior Jesus Christ. Amen."

"Thank you, sister," came the response as the immense column of pilgrims began to move again toward earth.

Carrie turned and began the return journey to Heaven, followed by her faithful brothers and sisters. Beautiful music reached their hearts once again as God their Father continued calling His children home. Home to the joy He had planned for them from the beginning.

"I tell you, in just the same way there will be more joy in heaven over one sinner who repents than over ninety-nine righteous people who have no need of repentance."
(LUKE 15:7, NAB)

For help in a crisis pregnancy,
call toll free:

1-800-848-LOVE (5683)

1-800-395- HELP (4357)

For help after an abortion,
call toll free:

1-877-HOPE-4-ME
(1-877-467-3463)

To order
Return of the Children
by John Regan

www.amazon.com

or

for a signed copy
with free shipping
contact the author:

johnregan2100@gmail.com

jreganjr@protonmail.com

About the author:

John Regan is a veteran pro-life worker, and a past president of Palm Beach County Right to Life League Inc. Having also served as President of Network for Re-Entry prison ministry, John has witnessed the healing effects of God's mercy and forgiveness in the lives of hundreds of incarcerated men and women. Inspired by those miraculous healings, he has sought to bring that same healing to those suffering from the effects of abortion. He created *Return of the Children* to touch the hearts of those who have been wounded by this national tragedy. In his professional life John was a radio news broadcaster, television weatherman, and business owner. John lives with his wife Joan, three daughters, eight grandchildren and four great grandchildren in Florida and can be contacted at:

johnregan2100@gmail.com
jreganjr@protonmail.com

About the illustrator:

Michelle R. Morse is a muralist and illustrator who is well-known in South Florida and across the Unites States for her colorful and whimsical murals and children's book illustrations. She has traveled on several mission trips to Honduras to paint murals in an orphanage and teach art to the orphans. She is also the illustrator of the award-winning DVD Family Time with Santa, winner of the 2005 Dove Award for best children's programming. In addition, she is the approved muralist for the Broward County (Greater Fort Lauderdale) school system. She has two adult children and one grandchild, and lives with her husband of forty years in Coral Springs, Florida. For more information, visit her Web site, www.mmorse.com .